HERE'S WHAT THEY'VE SAID ABOUT ANNE STUART!

ABOUT THE AUTHOR

Anne Stuart likes passionate stories and tales of love that transcend the experience of everyday life. She's also more than passingly fond of her "gorgeous husband and two wonderful children," not to mention her dog and four cats. A longtime contributor to Harlequin American Romance, Anne Stuart has warmed the hearts of readers worldwide.

Books by Anne Stuart

HARLEQUIN AMERICAN ROMANCE
93—HOUSEBOUND
126—ROCKY ROAD
177—BEWITCHING HOUR
213—BLUE SAGE
246—PARTNERS IN CRIME
260—CRY FOR THE MOON
311—GLASS HOUSES
326—CRAZY LIKE A FOX
346—RANCHO DIABLO
361—ANGEL'S WINGS
374—LAZARUS RISING
398—NIGHT OF THE PHANTOM
413—CHASING TROUBLE
434—HEAT LIGHTNING
453—RAFE'S REVENGE
473—ONE MORE VALENTINE
513—FALLING ANGEL
525—CINDERMAN
573—THE SOLDIER & THE BABY

HARLEQUIN INTRIGUE
9—CATSPAW
59—HAND IN GLOVE
103—CATSPAW II

Anne Stuart

A DARK &
STORMY NIGHT

Harlequin Books

TORONTO • NEW YORK • LONDON
AMSTERDAM • PARIS • SYDNEY • HAMBURG
STOCKHOLM • ATHENS • TOKYO • MILAN
MADRID • WARSAW • BUDAPEST • AUCKLAND

ISBN 0-373-16702-4

A DARK & STORMY NIGHT

Copyright © 1997 by Anne Kristine Stuart Ohlrogge

Printed in U.S.A.

Prologue

O'Neal stood alone, at the very edge of the cliff, and raised his face to the keening wind. The storm was coming, he could feel it coursing through his veins, throbbing in the very center of his bones. A huge, powerful storm that would sweep everything from the land with a furious hand, wipe everything clean.

He was ready for it. For fifteen years he'd lived a solitary life on the tiny spit of land jutting out into the North Atlantic, wandering around in the huge old stone mansion like the lost soul that he was. He had tried to escape countless times, but something always called him back, and he'd given up trying to figure out what it was. He only knew he belonged here. There was no peace for him, any-where in the world, but this remote piece of land on the coast of Maine was as close as he could come to acceptance. To peace.

Here he could be alone, alone with his past, alone with his future, alone with the strange curse that had torn his life apart. Here he could live out his days, doomed to solitude and the cold, salty embrace of the ocean.

Here he could endure, for as long as he had to. Until a storm too powerful to withstand swept him out to sea, and he would finally be free of the chains that bound him to this foreign land. This foreign life.

This curse.

Chapter One

October, hurricane season

Katie Flynn was a weather junkie. Much as it pained her to admit it, she loved storms and high winds, thunder and lightning, tornadoes and hurricanes and floods. Not that she actually delighted in the human misery such natural disasters caused. But there was a small, passionate part of her that got caught up in the wildness of nature. In something far bigger than mere human concerns.

She didn't go so far as to wish any of those disasters on hapless people. But if the storms and natural disasters were going to come, and common sense assured her that bad weather was a fact of life, then she enjoyed it with a vicarious pleasure soundly tinged with guilt.

However, she wasn't enjoying herself now.

She'd never actually been in the path of a hurricane before. Growing up in western Pennsylvania she'd been aware of them hovering, but apart from some heavier-than-usual rainstorms she hadn't been prey to the dangers of weather when she was younger.

Now she was smack-dab in the middle of nowhere with Hurricane Margo bearing down on her, and she was not a happy camper.

To be truthful, she wasn't exactly in the middle of nowhere. She was somewhere along the coast of Maine. She'd been traveling in a northeasterly direction for hours now, as the sky grew ominously darker and her cellular phone lost contact with the outside world, and she hadn't passed one of those tidy, white-painted little seaside villages for ages. Nor had she passed any cars. It was early October—too late for foliage tours, and besides, anyone with any sense would be tucked away in some nice safe motel.

Assuming the motels would be safe if the hurricane hit.

Katie should have stayed at the Lobster Pot Motel, glued to the Weather Channel and the increasing excitement. Instead she'd checked out, loaded her Subaru and headed into the grimly lit day. She'd promised herself she'd reach Bar Harbor and Mt. Desert Isle by evening, and she wasn't going to let the unlikely portent of a major hurricane get in her way. She liked to think of herself as practical and no nonsense, and getting into a tizzy over the possibility of a storm was a waste of time.

Much as she liked storms, she found they were

usually vastly overrated. They never hit where they were supposed to, there was always less snow or less rain, the winds died down, and the entire situation usually petered out in a depressingly unspectacular fashion. If she spent the day in the boxlike room at the Lobster Pot it was guaranteed that the storm would miss Maine entirely.

So here she was in the late afternoon, alone in her car, the cell phone dead, the radio a mass of static, the sky an eerie gray color and no one around for miles.

"You could have handled this better, Katie, my girl," she said out loud. She liked to talk to herself occasionally—it came from living alone. Not that she wanted it any other way. She was twenty-eight years old. Too old to be sharing an apartment, too young to be tied down in marriage to some ambitious young businessman. She liked her freedom and her solitude. She just wished she had a little company in her solitude at that moment.

At least the road was several miles away from the coast. If the hurricane hit, if it came with high surf and a storm surge, then she'd be miles inland. The road was paved, wide enough and deserted. Sooner or later she'd come to a town and a place to find shelter.

The crash echoed through the air like a blast of gunfire, and Katie slammed on the brakes in instinctive panic. Just in time to watch a huge tree crash down across the highway, thick branches splintering and skidding toward her small car.

She heard one connect with a solid thump, and she tried to shift into reverse, but the manual transmission had stalled out, and she was trapped, watching, as the huge old tree finally settled into a massive heap of trunk and limbs and brown leaves scudding away in the high winds.

"There's no way in hell I'm getting around that," she said in a flat voice. She climbed out of the car, peering through her wind-whipped hair as she checked for damages. The front tires were still sound, the fender only slightly dented from a flying piece of wood. There was no going forward, but she should have no trouble backing up. Just beyond the blocked roadway the highway seemed to widen, and she realized she was probably frustratingly close to civilization. But there was no way she could get past that tree, even with her four-wheel-drive vehicle.

She glanced at the shattered tree trunk, then froze, pushing the blinding tangle of hair from her eyes to stare more closely. Then she shook her head. For a moment she thought she'd seen someone in the branches of the tree. A girl in a long white dress with white-blond hair drifting down over her shoulders.

Oddly enough the hair and the clothes weren't blowing in the wind the way Katie's were. But of course, there was no one there—she knew that when she looked again. It must have been a trick of the eerie light, the strange weather descending on this barren stretch of coast.

She glanced behind her down the road. Retracing her steps lacked appeal, as well—she hadn't seen a house or a car for hours now, and the wind was picking up. That wasn't the only ancient tree that was going to topple in this kind of wind, and next time she might not be so lucky.

There was, however, a narrow dirt road leading off to the right, one she hadn't noticed before. She almost discounted it, then saw two mailboxes. If there were mailboxes, there were houses, and people. Even if the people were gone there would at least be shelter. The road probably led to a couple of small summer cottages. They might be closed up for the winter, but she'd have no compunction about breaking in and finding a safe harbor from the storm.

If she was lucky the road might lead around to whatever town lay ahead. Not that she was counting on any sudden gift of good luck. From her experience, once the day started going wrong it stayed that way, and this day was going very wrong indeed.

She was hungry, too—she'd planned to stop for lunch along the way, but she hadn't even seen a mom-and-pop grocery store to stock up on diet Coke and pretzels. She could only hope the summer people had left some canned food behind.

She started down the narrow road, driving slowly, her headlights making little dent in the afternoon gloom. At least it wasn't raining—she suspected the track would turn into a sea of mud with very little provocation. She realized she was gripping the steering wheel far too tightly, but she couldn't relax. It was no wonder, she told herself. This qualified as a high-stress vacation.

The road seemed to go on for miles, though Katie knew it was probably only her imagination and the snaillike pace she was forced to maintain. It was only four in the afternoon—far too early for it to be so dark, but maybe it had something to do with the fact that she was traveling east. There was definitely something creepy about the light.

And creepy about the tree toppling down right in front of her. Not to mention that wraithlike image she'd imagined. She reached down and turned on the radio, rewarded once again with an annoying crackle and an occasional word or two coming through the static. The tape player had eaten three tapes that morning, and she wasn't about to endanger Clannad or the Cranberries. It was bad enough to lose Elvis Costello to a haywire technology.

She decided to sing, very loudly, to chase her nervousness away. If the hurricane did choose to land on the coast of Maine, it wouldn't be hitting for another twenty-four to thirty-six hours, so she was silly to let it rattle her. There was no reason for her inexplicable sense of impending doom.

She sang "Ain't Misbehaving," and the rain began to splat down on her windshield. She went through a couple of other Fats Waller songs, then switched to old show tunes, always a convenient staple for long distance driving. She was halfway through "I Cain't Say No" when the car came to a fork in the road, and she paused, foot on the clutch this time, to decide which way to go.

To the left seemed the infinitely wiser choice. The road was wider and more traveled, and it headed back in the direction of the highway, probably circumventing the fallen tree. If she took the path to the right she'd be heading directly to the ocean, and the road was narrow, rutted and unpromising.

And then she saw the figure again. Like a ghost, flitting through the wind-tossed trees, it was just a flash of white like a sheet torn off someone's clothesline. Katie knew she should ignore it.

She also knew she wouldn't. She turned right, heading toward the ocean and the ghostly figure. Heading toward the storm.

She stopped when she got to the headlands, putting the car in neutral and climbing out, ignoring the fat drops of rain that splattered her. Shading her face, she peered northward, and through the swirling rain and wind she thought she saw an outcropping of land with a large building looming in the mist. It was huge—it looked like a school or a college, and Katie breathed a sigh of relief. Civilization. Fate was finally on her side. She was about to head back to the car when something caught her attention. She looked over the cliff, down into the roiling, angry sea, watching with fascination as it crashed against the rocks below. She stared, hypnotized, unable to move, and she found herself looking into a pair of eyes.

It was a seal, watching her from the rough waves, its brown head steady amidst the angry ocean. It was alone in that stormy froth, and Katie felt a sudden lurch of fear. If the storm grew wilder it could be dashed against the rocks and killed. Could seals drown? She had no idea, she only knew it looked deadly out there in the raging sea.

She wanted to call out to the creature, but the wind would have torn her voice and tossed it to the skies, and besides, what could she say? Shoo? Swim for your life? The seal would take care of himself.

As she needed to take care of herself.

She got back in the car and drove onward, into the darkness and the gathering rain, the headlights less than effective against the black storm. At least now she knew where she was heading. That large stone building would be proof against a hundred hurricanes, and it had seemed as if there was at least some light in the darkness. If she hurried she could reach safety before the fitful daylight disappeared entirely.

It wasn't the night to hurry. It wasn't the road to

hurry. The tires skidded in the deepening mud, the wipers couldn't keep up with the battering of rain. The huge old building loomed ahead of her, never getting any closer, and Katie found herself praying under her breath. "Please let me get there safely. Please let me get there *now*. Please." It didn't matter that she sounded like a whiny, impatient child in her mumbled entreaties. She was beyond dignity and well over the edge into truly pathetic need.

At last the road seemed to lead directly up to the huge stone building. It was smaller than she realized—it might be simply an old sea captain's mansion or a private school for wayward boys. That was all she needed at that point. A cadre of gang members to welcome her on a dark and stormy night.

She picked up speed, no longer caring about the condition of the road. She needed to stop driving, she needed food, she needed a bathroom, and she couldn't hold out much longer. She passed a gate, but the rain was coming down so heavily she couldn't see. The tires began to spin beneath her, and she pressed the gas pedal carefully. The car lurched ahead, and she was about to floor it when once again that white creature flitted across the rain-soaked windshield. And a young girl's face was staring at her.

Katie slammed on the brakes in panic, feeling the car slide forward through the mud, picking up speed despite her best efforts to stop it. She could see only darkness ahead of her, she could smell the sea, and she had the sudden, calm feeling that she was going to die.

The car slammed to an abrupt halt, and the sudden silence was shocking. The engine had stalled out once more, but the wipers were still dashing back and forth across the windshield, making little progress against the heavy downpour. The headlights speared out into rain and darkness, nothing more, and Katie sat there dazed, pushing the hair away from her face with a trembling hand as she tried to pull herself together.

"You're all right, Katie," she said aloud. It wasn't much of a comfort—her voice was shaking. "You'll just have to go for help." She opened the door and peered out, ready to step out into...

Nothingness. The car was perched at the edge of a cliff, the front-left tire hanging out over the stormy surf. Katie slammed the door again, cowering back into the car, only to have the lightweight vehicle sway beneath her. She couldn't stay where she was, but every movement she made seemed to make her perch more precarious.

"Don't move!" The wind caught a man's voice and swirled it toward her; for once in her life Katie was obedient. She didn't swing around abruptly to search for her rescuer—she allowed herself a brief, careful look in the rearview mirror. She could see the beam of a flashlight through the heavy rain but not much more.

She took a deep, calming breath. "What am I

supposed to do, then?'' she called out, trying to keep the asperity from her voice. "Just wait here until the car goes over the cliff?"

"Be quiet!" The voice was cool and clipped, and she wondered if she was imagining the faint Irish accent. "Willie's doing his best to secure your car, but we don't need you distracting us."

And she'd always had the fond belief that the Irish, the real Irish as opposed to her fourth-generation immigrant family, were charming. Nevertheless, if the ungracious creature was going to save her life, that would constitute charm enough, and she sat very still, watching the windshield wipers dash back and forth.

She felt the sudden lurch at the back of the car, and she swallowed a small scream as the vehicle shifted. If the unseen Willie was trying to secure her car he was doing a rotten job of it, and she was in no mood to head over the cliff with the Subaru as a coffin.

The car jerked again, and this time the little scream made it as far as her mouth. She bit it off, clenching the steering wheel tightly. As if it would do any good.

"All right, then," the disembodied voice came again, over the sound of the driving rain. "Open the door very slowly. You're going to need to move fast when I say the word, so be prepared."

Katie glanced back at the darkened interior of the car, wondering what she could grab. What did they say when an airplane crashed—you weren't supposed to take your purse, you were just supposed to run like hell?

She didn't even carry a purse, and her waist pack with her wallet was tossed somewhere in the back seat. But there was no way she was leaving her car without her beloved laptop computer.

"Open the damned door!"

She stopped thinking about her computer as the car lurched and settled again. She pulled the door handle, pushing against the door with extreme care. The wind was holding it closed, and she leaned her shoulder against it, only to have the car slide once more.

The door was yanked open from outside, and a tall, rain-shrouded figure reached out for her with strong hands. "Quickly now!" he shouted over the shrieking wind, pulling her.

The car began to slide over the cliff with a slow, rending groan, and Katie Flynn had left her seat belt fastened.

His curses were hurled toward the wind as he reached across her and struggled with the seat belt. Her own panicked hands were in the way, trying to release it, as well, and he slapped at her. All the while the car kept sliding inexorably downward.

"Hold on, Willie!" he shouted in a desperate voice.

"He can't hold on!" Katie shrieked back at him. "How can a man hold a car…?"

The seat belt released. The dark stranger hauled her out of the car with raw force, the sheer momentum sending the two of them tumbling into the mud. Katie lay beneath him, winded, as she heard the deep groaning sound that could only mean her car was finished.

The man rolled off her hastily, scrambling to his feet, but she lay there dazed for a moment as the heavy rain soaked her. She sat up in time to watch the taillights of her Subaru disappear over the cliff, pulling a heavy chain and a moderately sized tree with it.

"You're incredibly stupid, did you know that?" her rescuer said, looming over her. "We all could have been killed."

She looked up at him in the blinding rain, biting her lip. "Gallantry is clearly not your strong point," she said in her calmest voice.

She doubted it had any effect on him. He held out a hand for her, and much as she would have liked to disdain his aid she wasn't sure she could manage to get to her feet without it. She was feeling weak, shaken and, yes, very stupid indeed. Not that she was going to tell him so.

She put her hand in his, letting him haul her upright with an appropriate lack of grace. He released her immediately, and she did her best to control the slight wobble in her gait. "Do you want Willie to carry you?" he asked in that cool, disembodied voice.

She looked around her in the teeming darkness. She could only assume the massive, mountainous shape a few feet away was Willie, the man who had managed to keep her car from tumbling over the cliff for those much-needed moments. If he could hold a car he could probably carry her one-hundred-and-forty-five pounds of womanhood up to safety, but she wasn't about to chance it.

"I can walk," she said.

"Fine." Her less-than-charming hero turned his back on her and started up the slippery slope, leaving Katie with no choice whatsoever but to follow him as best she could.

Her sneakers slid in the mud, despite the state-of-the-art tread on their patented soles, and the rain had turned her into a drowned rat. Somewhere in her car was a raincoat, a heavy sweater, even an umbrella. Most likely the fishes would be enjoying them at the moment.

The huge stone building loomed before them, and Kate had the gloomy feeling it wasn't a nice safe school, or even a reformatory. The place was too dark, too deserted. But it was better than nothing, and she slogged through the deep puddles after her reluctant hero, concentrating on staying upright and keeping her teeth from chattering. She'd deal with her surroundings when she had to.

He pushed open a door, but the light from beyond was dim and unwelcoming. However, it had to be drier in there, even if it was dark and cold, and she didn't even hesitate, rushing past him only to stumble over the doorsill.

Bad luck, she thought. Katie Flynn enjoyed her superstitions, and she reached for the heavy gold cross that hung beneath her soaked shirt as an automatic protection. It was gone, and her sense of despair deepened. It was the one thing of value she owned, though its worth was more sentimental than anything else. It had belonged to her Irish great-grandmother, passed down through the generations, and its loss was a wound that left her bereft.

The door slammed shut behind her, and she was alone in the darkness, with him, her less-than-charming rescuer. And it seemed as if both of them were entirely incapable of polite conversation.

It would have been nice if she'd been a Victorian heroine. She was cold, frightened, thoroughly freaked-out by her near-death experience, and it would have been lovely to sink to the floor in a graceful faint.

Except that her host would have probably stepped over her body and abandoned her in this pitch-black hallway. And even an ungracious snot was better company than being alone in this strange place.

In the darkness her other senses were heightened, and she could smell the rain-soaked wool, the faint lure of brandy and wood smoke. If there was wood smoke clinging to him, then there must be a fire someplace. Warmth and brandy in this huge dark house, and she almost wept with longing.

She had the odd sense he could see her in the darkness, while she could focus on nothing more than a dark, looming figure. For a moment there was silence, broken only by the rush of the wind beyond the heavy door, and then he spoke.

"Come along, then," he said abruptly.

Not very welcoming. "Come along?" she echoed. "Where are we?"

"At the back side of hell," he replied. And he disappeared into the darkness.

Chapter Two

She made sloshing noises when she walked. The man ahead of her moved in absolute silence, but Katie squelched and squooshed as she hurried after him. She no longer worried about shivering—after all, the man might be able to see in the dark but he couldn't have eyes in the back of his head. And he very obviously didn't give a damn about her comfort.

It was gradually growing lighter as they moved through the dank, dark hallways of the huge old building, though her host blotted out most of the light. In truth, he wasn't that tall—probably around six feet, and Katie was used to tall men. He certainly wasn't bulky or overly muscled beneath the rain-soaked coat. But he seemed to absorb the light and warmth, keeping any from reaching Katie, and she wanted to reach out and grab his coat like an importunate beggar.

Instead she sneezed. Three times in a row, quite loudly. The man didn't even hesitate.

They must have climbed three narrow flights of stairs at the very least, traversed miles of hallway before they finally came out into a huge, dimly lit room. He halted, turning around to face her, but in the dim light she still couldn't see much more than his general shape.

"Don't you have electricity?" she asked, peering up at him through the darkness.

"Occasionally. Power supplies are temperamental out here, particularly when a hurricane is coming. Besides, we weren't expecting guests. Most sensible people stay put during this kind of weather."

"We've already figured out that I'm not sensible," she said. "I'm sorry I dragged you and your friend out in the rain. I'm sorry I nearly drove off a cliff. I'm sorry I was out driving when I should have been holed up in some hotel. I'm sorry I'm dripping all over your floor. I'm sorry I'm getting hysterical, but I'm cold and hungry and frightened and upset and I need a bathroom!"

He didn't move, didn't raise his voice, but the sound of it carried eerily through the cavernous room. "Mrs. Marvel!"

"Yes, sir?" The voice was surprisingly close, comfortable sounding. Katie felt some of her edginess fade.

"We have an unexpected guest," he said, moving away from her and stripping off his sodden raincoat. He moved to the fire, his back toward them

both. "Take her someplace to clean up, and see if
you can find her some dry clothes."

"Yes, sir. And how long will the young lady be
staying?" the woman asked with a strong Maine
accent.

"God knows," the man said wearily. "I suppose
it depends on the storm."

She obviously wasn't going to get a good look
at her less-than-charming host, so she turned and
flashed her most gracious smile at the woman
standing behind her. Mrs. Marvel looked just like
her voice—comfortable, elderly, warm and sensible.

"You look half-drowned, poor dearie," the
woman said. "You come along with me and we'll
see to your comfort. It must have been a terrible
fright for you. I'm just glad O'Neal and my Willie
heard you out there, or you would have been lost."

Katie shuddered, though she tried not to. She cast
a last, curious glance behind her at the tall, lean
figure of the man who must be O'Neal. He was
leaning against the mantel, staring into the fire, and
he'd obviously forgotten her existence.

She wanted to see his face. For some reason it
was terribly important, more important than getting
warm, even more important than a bathroom.

"O'Neal?" she said.

He looked up in surprise, across the shadowy
room, and she knew with sudden trepidation that
she'd made a very big mistake.

He was beautiful. There was no other word for it. His hair was long, dark with rain, pushed back from a face composed of planes and angles, features of such stark splendor that Katie was, for one brief moment in her determined life, struck dumb. Everything about the man was gorgeous, from his winged eyebrows, high cheekbones and narrow, strong nose, to his full mouth.

He was gay, she decided flatly. No one that good-looking was ever straight.

He was still looking at her, with deceptive patience, and the one thing she couldn't see clearly were his eyes. She was just as glad. "As you said, you're dripping on my carpet," he said in that cool, Irish voice that should have been charming. "If you want to stand there gawking like an idiot you may certainly do so, but I thought you needed a w.c."

His voice managed to startle her out of her trance. She spun around without a word, drops spraying from her rain-soaked clothes, and stomped off after Mrs. Marvel.

O'NEAL WATCHED HER GO. That was all he needed, he thought morosely. An unwanted visitor, a female, stuck for the duration of the storm. He could only rely on his hated instincts to guess how long this current blow would last, and for some reason he was having a difficult time reading his senses. The hurricane should blow itself out upon southern New England, giving them only a few days of high winds and lashing rains. Mrs. Marvel or her son could drive the tiresome creature into town in the morning, assuming things let up just the slightest bit. Even if it didn't, by daylight one of them could manage to drive at a slow crawl.

If worse came to worst, Willie could sling her over his back and carry her to Sealsboro. As long as he got her out of this house and away from him.

The heat from the fire slowly began to penetrate his bones, and he ran a hand through his long wet hair, pushing it back from his face. Stupid female, he thought. At least she hadn't screamed. The situation had been desperate enough, with that bloody car of hers hanging over the edge of the cliff. If she'd started yowling he would have been tempted to tell Willie to let the car tumble over.

And Willie, poor obedient soul, would have done it.

He needed hot, strong coffee, he needed a glass of brandy, he needed warm food, but most of all he needed his privacy. It was the worst time of all to be having an unwanted guest, but there was nothing he could do about it until morning. He could only hope Mrs. Marvel would have enough sense to keep the woman out of his way.

She'd looked like a drowned rat. A frightened, angry, slightly plump little rat, with her hair plastered to her pale face and her eyes huge and angry. He didn't want to see her when she was dried off.

He didn't want to see her or anybody else, if he could help it.

Unfortunately, fate, or the wicked guardian angel who seemed to delight in making his life a misery, seemed to have other ideas. The interloper was there, and there was nothing he could do about it but be as unwelcoming as he knew how to be. In hopes she'd be just as desperate to leave as he was to get rid of her.

Willie appeared in the doorway, his huge bulk filling it. "Where is she?" he asked in his deep, slow voice.

"Your mother's seeing to her comfort," O'Neal said. "Are you all right?"

Expressing concern for Willie's well-being was usually a waste of time, as it was now. He simply nodded, shuffling back into the darkness, and O'Neal went in search of the brandy. If he was going to have to see her again, at least he'd be well fortified.

KATIE DIDN'T BOTHER to ask how a house without electricity could manage to provide a hot shower. She didn't care—all she wanted to do was enjoy it. By the time she stepped from the steaming water her shivering had stopped, and she felt almost halfway human.

The clothes Mrs. Marvel provided her with were absurd, and Katie could only guess they came from her own closet. The gray skirt was so huge it settled low on Katie's ample hips, practically trailing along the floor, and the twin sweater set was vintage fifties and moth-eaten. But gloriously warm. She towel dried her hair as best she could, pulled on the thick kneesocks Mrs. Marvel had provided and went in search of the one friendly member of the household she'd met.

She wasn't alone in the cavernous kitchen. Seated at the table was a huge, silent creature that Katie immediately guessed was Willie. He looked to be in his late twenties, with a strange, slightly vacant expression on his broad face, which managed to be completely devoid of sweetness.

"You've already met my Willie," Mrs. Marvel said in her cheery voice. "The best son a mother could ever have. He's not too bright, but he's strong as an ox, and he always minds me. Don't you, Willie?"

He nodded, his eyes shifting over Katie and then skittering away. "Yes, Ma," he mumbled.

"Thank you for helping me earlier, Willie," she said in her most gentle voice. "You saved my life."

He looked up, and his eyes were flat and emotionless. "He doesn't want you here," he said. "He doesn't want anyone here. He should have left you out there if he didn't want you here."

"Willie!" Mrs. Marvel's voice carried a gentle warning. "You know O'Neal wouldn't begrudge anyone shelter from a storm, even if he's far from hospitable. Don't you pay Willie any mind, miss.

He gets a bit overzealous in trying to please O'Neal. And I, for one, am glad to have another woman's company for the night. It gets lonely with only a hermit and a—and Willie to talk with.''

Katie managed a smile in response. She'd had the oddest notion that Mrs. Marvel had been about to refer to her disabled son disparagingly, but she must have imagined it. The woman was looking at her son with a doting smile.

''You really think I'll be able to leave in the morning, Mrs. Marvel?'' she asked, as the wind whistled beyond the thick stone walls of the huge old house.

''I think O'Neal will see to it,'' she replied cheerfully. ''And what's your name? I don't want to keep calling you miss, now do I?''

''I'm Kathleen Bridget Moira O'Monaghan Flynn,'' she said. ''Most people call me Katie.''

''Irish!'' Mrs. Marvel said. ''Like O'Neal.''

''Generations removed from the Auld Sod,'' Katie said. ''It sounds like Mr. O'Neal is a new arrival.''

''Just O'Neal, dearie,'' Mrs. Marvel said. ''He doesn't like being called anything else. And he's not that recently come over. He's been in this house for the last fifteen years, and he hasn't left for more than a few days at a time.''

Katie stared at the older woman in disbelief. ''You're kidding!''

"On my honor," she said. "He seldom leaves, and no one ever comes to visit."

"But who else lives here?"

"No one. Willie and I have an apartment in the basement, but we're the only ones who come. O'Neal lives alone and likes it that way."

"But this house is huge!"

"And there's a guest house down the other way that's empty. I wanted to live there with Willie but O'Neal wanted it kept empty. He said it was too near the sea. Ridiculous, of course. This place is perched out on a spit of land with the sea all around it. The guest house is a good ways back. Ah, but who's to argue with the man when he's made up his mind? We're cozy enough here, Willie and me," she said comfortably. "I'll just need to find out where he wants me to put you for the night. There are a dozen empty bedrooms upstairs, but only a few of them have furniture, and I must admit, my dusting isn't what it should be in those deserted rooms."

"I don't blame you," Katie said. "I'm a devoted slob. I think housekeeping warps the brain."

"But, Katie," Mrs. Marvel said gently, "I'm a housekeeper by profession."

Put her foot in it that time, Katie thought. "I didn't mean—" she began, but Mrs. Marvel overrode her protests with cheery good sense.

"Don't worry about it," she said. "I'm not offended. Your generation is always so busy, it's no wonder standards have gotten a bit lax nowadays. And what is it you do for a living, Miss Katie? What brings you this far down east on a stormy October day?''

Katie made a face. "Let's just say I'm in the midst of a midlife crisis. I got sick of what I was doing, sick of living in cities, away from the ocean, away from nature. Things were just too fast paced for me. I decided I needed a career change, and I'm trying to find out what it is I want to do for the rest of my life. Where I want to live."

"You wouldn't want to live in a place like this," Mrs. Marvel said with absolute certainty. "It's one thing for the likes of Willie and me. And O'Neal's a hermit. He hates to be around people. But it's too quiet for a lively young thing like you."

"I don't know," Katie said with a sigh. "There are times when it seems like this rocky coast is exactly where I belong. I've never been a person who needs to be surrounded by other people. I need a certain amount of solitude."

"Don't you want to get married? Have children? Children are the joy of a woman's life." Mrs. Marvel cast a fond gaze at the oblivious Willie.

"People raise families in Maine. As a matter of fact, it seems like the best possible place for it."

"You wouldn't be happy here," Mrs. Marvel said with great certainty. "Take my advice, dearie. Marry a rich man. There's nothing better than a pile of money."

"I wouldn't know," Katie said, glancing around her. "I've never had any to spare."

"Neither have I, but I can guess," Mrs. Marvel said. "Too often money is wasted on those who don't appreciate it. Like O'Neal. Ah, but then, no one ever said life is fair, did they?" she said with a hearty sigh. The sound of a tiny, musical bell interrupted them. "That's himself. You'd best come with me and we'll see what he wants to do with you."

"Won't I have some say in the matter?" Katie responded with a trace of humor.

"No," said Willie morosely from his spot at the table. He looked up at her, and his eyes were bleak and dark and soulless.

And Katie found there was still a stray shiver in her newly warmed body.

She didn't even see him in the room when she followed Mrs. Marvel back. The fire was blazing gloriously beneath the heavy marble mantel, casting eerie shadows about the huge room, but O'Neal was nowhere to be seen. Until she heard his voice emanating from one corner.

"Did you feed her?"

"No, sir. I thought you'd be wanting her to eat with you."

Katie half expected him to say "Why would I want that?" in his chilly Irish voice, but he said nothing, emerging from the shadows with slow grace.

"When's supper?"

"Half an hour. And what room would you be wanting me to put her in?"

"It doesn't matter. Wherever you see fit," he said.

Katie was not enjoying herself. She had a temper to go with her red hair, and she hated being talked about as if she weren't even in the room.

She took a step toward him. "I don't want to be a bother."

"It's too late for that," he said coolly. "If you didn't want to be a bother, you shouldn't have tried to drive over the cliff."

"I didn't! It was an accident." She was beginning to find Mr. Brooding-Master-of-the-Mansion O'Neal to be highly annoying. "If that damned ghost hadn't popped in front of my window..."

She hadn't meant to say that. The temperature of the room dropped ten degrees, and the man opposite her, still shrouded in shadows, seemed to turn to ice.

"You believe in ghosts, Miss...?"

Oddly enough, it was a question, not another accusation of stupidity. "Flynn," she said. "Katie Flynn."

"Oh, God," he murmured. "Irish."

"Indeed," she said. "And would you be having anything against the Irish?"

He came out of the shadows. He'd changed, as well, and he was wearing faded jeans and a thick wool sweater against the damp chill of the room. His long hair had dried, and it was the deep, rich brown of a seal, so thick and lustrous that some foolish woman would want to put her hands on it. Fortunately Katie Flynn was no fool.

He raised his head to look at her, letting his eyes run over her body with cool disinterest, but Katie was beyond caring. She knew what she looked like in her bulky, hand-me-down clothes, and besides, vanity was not one of her many weaknesses.

She was too busy staring at his eyes in wonder. They were the color of the sea—there was no other way to describe them. Green and blue and stormy, translucent, deep and endless, they touched her and she was lost. There was no fairness in a world that would give a man a glorious face and present him with such mesmerizing eyes as well.

"I left Ireland to get away from the Irish," he said.

"You came to the wrong country then," she shot back. "We're all over the place."

"Most people leave me alone out here."

"Aren't you lucky that I'm here to break your boredom?"

He paused, startled. "I beg your pardon?"

"And you can give me a glass of that brandy," she said, taking the bull by the horns. "And I think if you try to exert yourself you could probably manage to be pleasant long enough for me to eat dinner. And then I promise I'll go away to whatever attic room you intend to lock me in. I'll leave first thing in the morning and you'll never have to be bothered with me again," she said. "But in the meantime I'm not in the mood to replay *Wuthering Heights* or *Jane Eyre*, I don't want you glowering at me, and if you can't manage to be pleasant I can always eat in my room."

He stared at her, clearly unimpressed. "Mrs. Marvel hasn't had time to prepare a room for you. And your hair's still wet. Go sit by the fire, and I'll see if I can find another brandy snifter. I'm not used to guests."

"I never would have dreamed." Like most strong-willed, cantankerous creatures, O'Neal seemed to respond best to a firm hand. He was rather like a huge, Maine coon cat she'd once been owned by. Puska had muscled his way into her life, simply showing up one morning at the farmhouse where she was staying. He'd bullied her, tormented her, graciously allowed himself to be fed and petted when the mood struck him and had done his best to run her life. It had been a permanent battle, and when he'd finally died of old age she'd mourned for months.

She didn't want to be thinking of Puska, or anything that made her vulnerable. Instead she headed for the fire, sinking down on the floor in front of it and shaking the excess water out of her hair. "What is this place?" she asked, busy trying to finger comb her hair.

A brandy snifter appeared in front of her, held in one particularly elegant hand. For a moment she didn't move, caught by the beauty of his hand, the long fingers cupping the globe of the snifter. He had to be gay, she thought morosely.

She took the glass, careful not to touch him, but it was warm from his hand, and the sensation was unnerving. "It's a house," he said, moving away from her with unflattering haste.

"I mean, what did it used to be? Who lived here before you did?"

"I gather it was built in the 1800s by some wealthy ship owner. It's had a checkered history— it was a school for a time, and a private sanitarium."

"You mean like for TB patients?"

"Not in this damp climate, Katie Flynn. It was a private mental clinic. If we look we can probably find some old straight jackets in the attic."

"Not *Wuthering Heights*," she muttered. "*Jane Eyre.*"

"I have no mad wives in the attic, I assure you. And as long as you behave yourself I won't have Willie lock you up."

He was probably being facetious, but it was hard to be certain. She took a sip of the brandy, savoring the warmth as it slid down her throat. "Don't you have any family?" she asked.

It was the wrong question, but she'd already accepted the fact that in O'Neal's presence she could do no right. "They're dead. Drowned in the deep salt sea, every one of them."

Unbidden, the memory of her car, tumbling over the cliff into the black and roiling ocean, came back to haunt her. "I'm sorry," she said.

"Don't be," he dismissed her sympathy rudely. "It was fifteen years ago. I got over it."

"Not if you've been a hermit ever since."

He moved closer, and he clearly wasn't pleased. Katie took another hasty sip of her brandy. "Mrs. Marvel has been talking," he said, and there was no lilt in his Irish voice. "And you've been prying."

She tilted her head back to look up at him, way up the length of him as he towered over her. He was probably trying to intimidate her, an easy enough thing since she was sitting on the floor, but Katie Flynn wasn't a woman who was easily intimidated.

"Chill out, Mr. Rochester," she said flatly. "There's nothing wrong with simple human curiosity."

"I'm not a romantic hero," he snapped.

"I'm more than aware of it. You may be pretty but your personality could use some major improvement." She took a deep breath, then shook herself. "Sorry. I get carried away sometimes. I guess you're wishing you let me tumble into the sea."

"No," he said. "I wouldn't wish that on anyone.

Even you." He stared down at her. "You have blue eyes. Very Irish blue eyes."

"So?"

"Mary Mother of God, your hair is red, isn't it?" He sounded truly horrified by the notion.

"All natural," she responded in an exaggeratedly perky voice. "And I've got pale skin and freckles. I'm Irish. I'm superstitious. I'm feisty. So what's it to you?"

He stared at her, a lost look in the back of his eyes. "Nothing but trouble, Katie Flynn. Nothing but trouble."

Chapter Three

Dinner was conducted in almost complete silence. Willie served them, and the food was heavenly, but Katie's few attempts at initiating conversation were met with monosyllabic answers or nothing at all.

"You know," she said, determined to lighten the atmosphere, "this is probably the first time since I've been in Maine that I haven't had seafood for dinner."

"I eat enough fish," O'Neal said.

"Oh, I'm not complaining," Katie said hastily. "This chicken is delicious. I was just surprised—"

"Do you always prattle?" he interrupted her.

"When I'm the only one making dinner conversation, yes," she said.

"Have you ever heard of eating in peace?"

"Is that like resting in peace?"

He flinched, and belatedly she thought of his family, all drowned in the rough ocean. It must have been in a storm like this one, she thought. No wonder he was less than cheerful.

"I'm sorry," she said. "I'll be quiet."

"Good."

She preferred not to look at him. His fine-boned face was distracting, disturbing to her. She had never reacted to male beauty in such a way. She was not a vain woman, and tended to respond to people's behavior, not their looks. The few men she'd been even slightly involved with had been ordinary enough, and she'd never even been particularly vulnerable to movie-star crushes.

But O'Neal was different. It was more than mere good looks, though he had them in abundance. There was something mesmerizing about him, something that called to her, something that had nothing to do with a pretty face and everything to do with a lost soul.

She shook herself mentally, concentrating on the hot rolls Mrs. Marvel had provided, rather than on her host. She needed to remember the old adage: Handsome Is As Handsome Does. Judged by those standards, O'Neal was a troll.

The housekeeper appeared the moment Katie put down her fork, and she wondered whether the woman had been watching, or if O'Neal himself had managed some unseen, unheard signal. "You'll be wanting to get some sleep, now, won't you dearie," she cooed, sounding bizarrely like Mrs. Doubtfire. "My, but you've a sturdy appetite. It's a treat cooking for someone other than O'Neal...he just picks at his food."

It was a dubious compliment at best, but O'Neal seemed oblivious. He'd already turned away from her, watching the fire through slitted eyes, dismissing her.

"It would be hard not to do justice to such delicious food," she managed, pleased with herself.

Was that a faint curve in O'Neal's perfectly chiseled lips? Surely the man was devoid of humor. He wouldn't be likely to find her fast comeback amusing.

It must have been wishful thinking on her part. Still, she'd been well brought up, and she needed to remember her manners. "Mr. O'Neal—" she began.

Whatever lightening in his mood vanished immediately. "It's O'Neal," he said. "No *mister*."

She wanted to smack him. Instead she rose, dropped her linen napkin on the table and summoned up a cool smile. "Thank you for your hospitality," she said.

He didn't bother to look at her, as if he found the sight of her disturbing. "You'll want to be leaving here as early as you can, I'm sure. I won't be seeing you in the morning, but Mrs. Marvel will drive you into Sealsboro and help you see about replacing your car."

There wasn't much she could say in response to that, but Mrs. Marvel filled the gap. "And glad I am to do it," she said. "You come along with me, dearie. I've fixed up one of the nicest bedrooms, and Willie's got a fire going. The electricity is out again, but you'll be wanting a good night's sleep. There's no television in the house, anyway, even if we had the power to run such a thing."

"What about a telephone?" she asked belatedly.

"O'Neal doesn't hold with such things. He thinks they're an intrusion on his privacy."

"Like me," Katie said.

"Like you," O'Neal agreed in a sepulchral voice from the wing chair in front of the fire. "Goodbye, Miss Flynn."

He couldn't see her, and Katie had had enough. "Good night, O'Neal," she said. And stuck her tongue out at him.

DAMN THE GIRL. Damn her red hair and her freckles and her fearless blue eyes. Damn her temper and her luscious body and her wicked, cruel luck in finding her way to Seal Point.

And damn him, for not being able to ignore her, no matter how hard he'd tried.

It wasn't as if she was the first pretty girl who'd wandered into his life. He'd been able to resist the others, just as he would resist Katie Flynn. But there was something about her that got beneath his skin.

He laughed grimly. A perfect turn of phrase. Beneath his skin indeed. And which skin was it, he wondered? The smooth white flesh that covered him now. Or...?

He didn't want to think about it. Didn't want to think about the night, the ocean crashing in huge waves as the storm flirted with the Atlantic Coast. He didn't want to think about looking up in the darkness and seeing her, standing on the headland, looking down into the sea. Down into his eyes.

He wanted to get drunk. He made it a habit to watch the amount of brandy he drank; he had no desire to drink himself to death. It was too depressing and undignified. If he did choose to end this half life, he'd simply head out to sea one day.

It was going to happen, sooner or later. The solitude was driving him mad. But there was no other choice, given who and what he was. The curse of the O'Neals haunted him, and there was no escaping it.

Not in the blue eyes of a creature who should have been washed out to sea like his family, so long ago. Not in her arms and the soft promise of her sweet body.

There was no escape, and Katie Flynn's blue eyes and red hair only reminded him of how much he wanted to.

Damn her.

THE PLACE was a gothic castle at its best. Mrs. Marvel settled her into the corner bedroom with a pile of quilts and the warning to get as much sleep as she could. The heat from the blazing fire barely penetrated the cavernous room, and even the voluminous flannel nightgown she'd been given wouldn't be much help. Katie changed clothes quickly, crawled into the huge old bed and lay there, shivering, staring at the candle that she had absolutely no intention of blowing out.

Automatically she reached for the cross that usually hung around her neck, and once more she felt the loss deep in her heart. It was silly to become so attached to physical things, but she couldn't help it. The cross was her family, her heritage. And it was now at the bottom of the sea.

She closed her eyes, trying to relax. Her entire body was a mass of aches, though she wasn't quite sure why. When O'Neal had hauled her out of the car moments before it went crashing into the sea he'd been rough, and she could still feel the jolt of his bones as they'd slammed into hers when they'd tumbled onto the ground. But still, it wasn't as if she'd actually been hurt. And he…and he…

She sat bolt upright in the frigid room, listening to the wind howl outside the leaded-glass windows. "Oh, my God," she said out loud. Miss Katie Flynn, well-brought-up daughter of Charles and Maggie Flynn, had thanked her rescuer for dinner and a bed for the night. She'd forgotten the tiny issue of saving her life.

She scrambled out of bed, cursing beneath her breath. The floor was icy beneath her bare feet, she could almost see her breath in the frigid room, and there was no sign of either the clothes she came in or the clothes she borrowed. Mrs. Marvel had said her own clothes would be dry by the morning, so she must have taken her own baggy stuff with her. Leaving Katie stuck in the room with nothing but a tentlike flannel nightgown to wear.

She ought to go back to bed. O'Neal had dismissed her with his lordly manner, making it clear he had no intention of ever seeing her again. It was his fault that she wasn't able to thank him for the small favor of saving her life.

She could write him a thank-you note once she made it safely back to civilization. That was the sensible thing, and the least intrusive on her unfriendly host. She should jump back in bed, pull the covers over her and plan to handle her social obligations in absentia.

She didn't move, ignoring the fact that she was as cold as hell. She wasn't getting back in that bed—she wouldn't sleep until she'd taken care of the matter. It didn't matter that he'd probably throw something at her if she intruded on his solitude one more time. It didn't matter that all she had to wear was a nightgown the size of a small tent. It didn't even matter that she'd probably never find her way back to that cavernous room through the dimly lit mazelike corridors of this old house. She wasn't going to get a wink of sleep unless she at least tried to complete the unpleasant, self-imposed task.

There was no reason for a house to be so cold this early in October, she thought miserably as she made her way down the narrow hallways. Any more than she should be plagued with the annoying memory of someone once telling her that it was always cold when there were ghosts present. Katie was superstitious, but she wasn't a fool. She didn't really believe in ghosts, goblins, demons or things that went bump in the night. That white apparition that kept appearing was nothing more than a stray wisp of fog, or a piece of litter, or one of a dozen other possibilities.

And the huge old house was cold because it was made of stone, there was no central heating, the night was windy, she was barefoot.... There was always a reasonable explanation if you chose to look for it.

Astonishingly enough she made no wrong turns in her quest for the cavernous room where she'd left O'Neal. She made no sound at all with her chilled bare feet, and when she came to the open door she stopped, peering inside. The fire had burned down, there were no candles lit, and the entire room seemed shadowy, almost haunted.

But she didn't believe in ghosts, she reminded herself.

She couldn't see around the back of the wing chair. He might be there, or he might not. He might have fallen asleep watching the fire, and he wouldn't welcome her waking him up. Or he might be dead....

Stop it, she ordered herself sternly. *You're letting your imagination run wild.*

She tiptoed into the room, ready to turn and run at the first warning. She moved toward the chair in silence, peering around, only to find it empty. He was gone.

She let out a deep sigh of disappointment mixed with relief. At least she'd tried. She turned, and he was there, watching her out of those sea-storm eyes.

She screamed, unable to help herself, and she half expected him to clamp a hand across her mouth. He didn't touch her, didn't come any closer to her. He was close enough.

"What the hell are you doing here?" he demanded. "I thought I'd gotten rid of you."

"What a charming thought," Katie said when her heart started beating again.

"What do you want? If you're looking for more food, Mrs. Marvel keeps the kitchen well stocked. If you're looking for brandy, take the bottle and be gone. If you're looking for companionship I'm not the one to provide it."

"I should say you're not," she retorted, incensed. "I came to thank you."

"Thank me?"

"For saving my life. I forgot to earlier, and since I didn't expect to see you again I wanted to make sure I had a chance to thank you."

"Believe me when I say it was nothing."

It was the final straw. Her feet were blocks of

ice, her entire body was racked with shivers, and he was looking down his elegant nose at her as if she were a rabid chipmunk.

"You are the nastiest son of a bitch I have ever met in my entire life," she said in a rush, unable to restrain herself any longer. "It's a lucky thing for you that you're a hermit—if you spent any time around normal people they'd probably kill you."

She was unprepared for his bitter laugh. "Truer words than you know, Katie Flynn," he said. "And yes, I'm a son of a bitch, and we both know it. If you have any sense at all you'll run back to your bedroom, lock the door and hope you never see me again."

All her anger had vanished. She realized then that he'd been drinking. He wasn't precisely drunk, but he'd had enough brandy to add a glitter of recklessness to his green eyes.

"But why?" she said, distracted, when she knew she should leave. "What have I ever done to you?"

"Besides dragging me out in a monstrous storm and nearly pulling me into the sea with you? Besides invading my house and my life?"

"Yes, besides that." She was entirely uncowed.

He came right up to her, too close, and caught her face in his hands. Beautiful, elegant hands, framing her face as he stared down at her, almost as if he were trying to memorize her features.

"You have red hair and blue eyes, Katie Flynn," he said in a soft voice that sent an odd little shiver down her spine. "You have a good soul and a fierce heart, and you remind me of everything I can't have in this life. You're too bold and too pretty, and the more I see of you the more you'll haunt my dreams. Now run back to your room before I kiss you."

She was frozen, staring up at him in disbelief. He was standing so close to her that his clothes were brushing the tentlike nightgown, and she wanted to sink against him, to feel his arms around her, to feel his body pressed up against hers. She wanted to see if his beautiful mouth would taste any different from the ordinary mouths of mortals.

He leaned forward, and she let her eyes flutter closed, unable to stop him, unable to resist the shocking temptation of him. His lips gently touched her eyelids, then her temples, where the blood was pounding. But he didn't kiss her mouth.

Instead he drew back, releasing her, and his eyes were bleak and endless. "Run away, Katie Flynn," he whispered. "Before I drown you."

SHE RAN, as he knew she would. She ran as if the devil was after her. Little did she know the devil was staying behind, his last ounce of decency keeping him from following her.

He'd wanted her mouth with a hunger that wrenched him apart. He'd wanted the warm, supple curves of her body; he'd wanted to touch her and taste her and take her, over and over again.

It was the brandy, he told himself. It was the

solitude. It was the woman herself, and he knew it. She was all his fantasies rolled into one; erotic, romantic, foolish and impossible. He could resist her, he could resist his own crazy longings. He'd made it through the past fifteen years, he could make it through however long he had left, be it fifteen or fifty.

He sank down in the wing chair, staring into the fire. He didn't dare touch another drop of the brandy. It had already managed to peel away his defenses enough so that he'd touched her. It was small consolation that he hadn't kissed her mouth. If he had one more glass of brandy he would go after her and finish the job. He wouldn't be stopping at kissing.

He leaned back, closing his eyes, clenching and unclenching his fists. He could almost feel the ocean surging around him, buoyant, supporting him, rocking him. He needed to concentrate on that peaceful rocking, putting all thoughts of Katie Flynn and mortal females out of his mind.

But he knew, with desperate certainty, that from that day on his erotic fantasies wouldn't be of willowy creatures in lacy negligees. They would be of Katie Flynn in a flannel nightgown, warm skin beneath the soft cotton. They would be of Katie Flynn.

"WILLIE, MY BOY," Mrs. Marvel said gently, "I'm very disappointed in you."

"I know, Ma," he mumbled, ducking his head.

"What have we been working for? These long long years, we've come so close, and it could all be ruined. You know that, don't you, son?"

"Yes, Ma."

"She's a pretty girl, isn't she?" Mrs. Marvel came up behind her son, kneading his thick shoulders with her strong, strong hands. "You've always liked pretty girls, haven't you, Willie?"

"I didn't touch her, Ma!" His voice rose in sudden panic. He tried to turn around and face her, but her grip was too strong, holding her huge son in place more by the force of her personality than the strength in her hands. "I promised I wouldn't ever again. Not unless you tell me I can. I'll do what you tell me, I promise."

"I know you didn't touch her. You're a good boy, you always do just what your mother tells you."

"Yes, Ma," he said, sniffling.

She patted his shoulders comfortingly and stepped away. "That's my Willie," she murmured.

He glanced up at her with a worried expression on his dull face. "He wanted her, too, you know."

"I know, Willie," she said softly, taking her seat at the table and reaching for the whiskey bottle. It was O'Neal's best Irish whiskey, and she was unstinting with herself and her son. "But he wouldn't touch her. I can count on that much. You know what you should have done, don't you?"

"Yes, ma'am."

She nodded sagely. "There's no harm done, though. I'll take her into town tomorrow and get rid of her. She'll forget all about this place, and O'Neal, and we'll be back as we were, safe and cozy."

Willie looked troubled. "Do you think the rain will stop, Ma?"

"For her sake she'd better hope so. Otherwise we'll be forced to take drastic steps."

Willie hunched lower in his seat. "Can I do it, Ma?"

"You failed me once, boy. Why should I give you the pleasure?" his mother asked sternly.

"I won't make another mistake, I promise you, Ma. Let me prove myself. Please, Ma. I won't let you down this time, you know I won't."

Mrs. Marvel looked at her son with a fond, mother's glance, considering the alternatives. Then she nodded. "All right, Willie. If the rain keeps up you can kill her. Just don't make it take too long, all right? We're not supposed to take pleasure in another human's misery. Haven't I brought you up right?"

"Yes, Ma," said Willie. And he smiled happily.

Chapter Four

The small cool hands that touched her face were
not the hands of O'Neal. Even in her dream she
knew that. She lay very still in the huge bed, huddled beneath the mound of covers, her eyes shut
against the cocooning darkness. The fire had gone
out hours ago, the candle had burned to the socket,
and outside the rain lashed against the window, the
wind howled, and the ghost knelt on her bed and
touched her face.

Katie opened her eyes then, knowing what she
would see. It was the ghost girl, with her long
white-blond hair and her sweet face. She said something, but Katie could hear no words, just the sound
of the sea all around her.

Fiona, she was. Katie knew that without hearing
it. She had come for a reason, she had brought Katie
there for a reason, but for now there were no words
to tell it. She put her hands on Katie's, the touch
cool and light as a gull's wing, and on her pale
small hand was a golden ring set with a stone the

color of the sea, green and stormy. The color of O'Neal's eyes.

And then she was gone. The room was still cold, dispelling the myth that it was ghosts who brought the cold. And Katie closed her eyes once more and slept.

"THERE YOU ARE, dearie," Mrs. Marvel greeted her warmly. "I've made some fresh muffins and oatmeal, and there's coffee in the pot over there, nice and strong. How did you sleep, then?"

In the murky, storm-laden daylight the kitchen was warm and welcoming, a fitting setting for the coziness of Mrs. Marvel. Kate managed a convincing stretch. "Very well indeed," she said, ignoring the nightmares and the chill and the howl of the wind outside her room. "Thank you for bringing my clothes."

"Well, I knew you wouldn't be wanting to wear my old things any longer than you have to," she replied, setting a plate of muffins on the table in front of her. "As soon as you're finished breakfast we'll set out."

Katie glanced toward the high-set windows of the basement kitchen. "Do you think we'll be able to make it into town?"

"Certainly," the housekeeper said briskly. "I was born and bred Down East—I'm not about to let a little storm stop me. And I'm sure you want to get back to civilization as quickly as you can."

She poured two cups of coffee and joined her at the table. "Have you decided what you're going to do?"

"I don't have much choice, considering my purse and all my identification and credit cards are now resting on the bottom of the Atlantic Ocean. When we get to town I'll call my parents and have them wire me some money. How far is the nearest airport?"

"Oh, quite a ways, dearie. But don't worry, I'm sure Lemuel will be willing to drive you there for a reasonable sum of money. With any luck you'll be home by tonight. Though the sooner we get on the road the better." Mrs. Marvel glanced toward the storm-shrouded windows. "There's no telling what's going to happen with the storm, and we want to get you back home as quickly as possible, now, don't we?"

Katie wasn't particularly convinced of that, but she nodded. "Is the hurricane coming?"

The housekeeper shrugged her plump shoulders. "Who's to say? We don't even have a battery radio out here. O'Neal doesn't like civilization intruding. When we get to town we'll find out the latest."

"I wouldn't want you to get stranded."

Mrs. Marvel smiled her cozy smile. "Don't you worry, dearie. I'm very good at taking care of myself. Why don't you bring your coffee with you? Willie brought the car around earlier, and I don't think it would be wise to wait any longer."

She didn't want to leave. It hit her with the force of a blow, shocking her. The strange dreams, the even stranger man and the gathering storm all held her there in that huge old mausoleum of a place, and she hated the thought of turning her back on it all, of running away.

She couldn't very well invite herself to stay. Even if it somehow seemed she was meant to. She rose, pushing away from the table. "That's all right," she said briskly. "I don't need any more coffee. I need to see what I can do about replacing my car."

"I hope you didn't have anything too valuable in there?"

Katie shook her head. "Just clothes, a few tapes. My laptop. And my purse...." Her voice trailed off as she thought of her grandmother's cross, lost forever.

"What's wrong, dearie?"

Katie shook her head, fighting the absurd urge to cry. "Just an old cross that had once belonged to my grandmother. It must have come off in the car. I shouldn't fuss—it only had sentimental value and not much more."

"Well, you escaped with your life and your health," Mrs. Marvel said. "Those are the most important things. Even if you can't replace the cross, you'll still have the memories, won't you?"

Katie managed to smile. It was a weak effort, but Mrs. Marvel accepted it at face value. "And you never can tell, O'Neal may be able to find it in the spring," Mrs Marvel continued. "He's done some diving and some salvage work. You be sure to write us when you get settled, and if anything turns up we'll send it to you."

It was a faint hope, but Katie was willing to grasp at anything. "That would be wonderful," she said. "It was gold. I don't know how the salt water would affect it...."

"Oh, gold's just about indestructible. You should see some of the artifacts O'Neal has brought up from the ocean floor. He'll find your grandmother's cross, I'm certain of it."

"I doubt he'd want to bother."

"Now, dearie, O'Neal isn't as unfriendly as he seems. He's just a little standoffish."

Out of the blue she felt it again, the whisper-soft brush of his lips against her eyelids, her temples. "Unfriendly isn't the right word," she said in a strained voice. "He's...odd."

"Yes, he's very odd. It comes from living alone for so long, with no family. It comes from the sadness in his life," Mrs. Marvel said. "Best leave the poor man in peace, Katie Flynn." She took a heavy black raincoat from a peg near the door and began to bundle up. "He's earned his rest."

Katie's raincoat was with everything else, at the bottom of the ocean. She wondered if O'Neal could be talked into salvaging that, as well—it cost her a fortune that she could no longer afford. "Then I'll leave him to it,'' she said firmly, banishing the memory of his haunted eyes.

O'NEAL STOOD in the window, watching them leave. The storm had abated just slightly, a small mercy from an angry providence, and Mrs. Marvel and the interloper took off into the gray day at a brisk pace.

He pulled back, telling himself it was relief he felt and nothing more. The temptation had been removed, and he hadn't even kissed her. She would likely tell tales of the strange man she met in the midst of a nor'easter, but since she would be miles, states away, it wouldn't matter. And she hadn't been there nearly long enough to even begin to guess his secret.

The Marvels had served him, lived with him in this empty shell of a house, for more than twelve years, and even they had no inkling of the truth. Probably they wouldn't believe it even if they saw the proof of it with their own eyes. They had no Irish blood in them—they were stern, pilgrim stock with no imagination or music in their souls. They wouldn't believe in folk tales or curses or ancient legends.

He wouldn't believe them, either, if he hadn't been forced to live one out. And the only music in his soul nowadays was a requiem.

He would drink lots of strong black coffee, he told himself, and read. He read voraciously—anything he could get his hands on. Textbooks and murder mysteries and scientific treatises and comic books. He loved the feel of paper and the printed word. The one thing he loved that had no place in the sea.

What in heaven's name had she been babbling about? The white ghost that had led her to invade his solitude and almost killed her. He supposed he believed in ghosts, of course, even though he'd never seen one. He'd be a fool not to.

But ghosts were harmless creatures, appearing for a purpose and then quickly gone. They didn't lure innocents to their deaths.

Innocents to their deaths. The words rang through his consciousness like a dirge. How many people had died? Innocent people he had loved so dearly. And he hadn't been able to save them.

He'd saved Katie Flynn, though. That should count against his sins. Except that he knew full well that he was the one who judged himself so harshly. And nothing would wipe out the memory of that night fifteen years ago.

The wind gusted suddenly, slamming against the leaded-glass windows of the library, rattling the panes. He heard the huge, groaning noise from a great distance, with his soul rather than his ears, and he froze. Not for one moment did he believe Katie and Mrs. Marvel were dead—life didn't work that way. But whatever that noise was, it had stopped Katie Flynn from leaving his life. Fate had more tricks to play on him.

He looked out into the dark morning, but the rain was coming down in such torrents now, the wind driving it against the windows, that he could barely see. He could leave them there, to find their way back to the house, or over the edge of the cliff if that was their fate. Or he could head out once more into the storm and find them. Find her.

Willie was nowhere to be seen when O'Neal ducked out into the rain. The Range Rover was still in the garage, but the Volvo station wagon was gone. Mrs. Marvel preferred luxury cars, though this time she might have made the wrong choice. The slick mud underfoot called for all the automotive advantage available.

The headlights made little dent against the rain, and he drove slowly, squinting, looking for any sign of movement that could be human. He was probably crazy for going out in this mess. There was a good chance he'd imagined that sound, and his overwrought mind had done the rest. He hadn't slept well, he'd had too much to drink, and Katie Flynn had upset his dubious equilibrium. And now he was chasing after ghosts in a storm, just as his unwanted visitor had done.

He slammed on the brakes, ready to turn back. Mrs. Marvel was an impressive creature—she was more than capable of taking care of herself and whatever stray creatures turned up.

He shifted the Rover into reverse, and the gears ground with an ominous shriek. He glanced up, and through the pounding rain he saw a flash of white.

It was nothing, he told himself. A seagull trying to force its way through the punishing headwinds, a piece of newspaper picked up by the storm. But he shifted back into first gear, smoothly this time, and began to creep forward once more.

The storm lessened with a suddenness that was shocking, and he hit the brakes once more, skidding in the mud before he brought the Rover to a halt. The Volvo lay beneath a huge tree, its hood crushed, windshield shattered. There was no sign of its occupants.

The roar of the wind drowned out any sound as he leaped from the car and slammed the door behind him. He called out a name, no longer caring that it was Katie he called for, not his loyal housekeeper.

He found them in a ditch on the far side of the road. Katie lay still and pale, and the housekeeper was leaning over her with tender solicitousness.

"Mrs. Marvel!" he called out, and she turned, dropping the large rock she held in her hand.

"Thank God you're here, sir!" she cried earnestly. "She's been hurt, and there was no knowing how I could get her back to the house."

O'Neal had already reached them. He touched Katie's pale, still figure. Her heartbeat was steady, her pulse strong, but the gash on her forehead was oozing blood.

He knew enough about head wounds to remember that they always bled wildly. He knew enough about head wounds to realize she could either be dying from a crushed skull or suffer only a minor headache. Once again fate was playing a malicious hand, upping the ante.

She opened her eyes, blinking as the rain splattered her face, and it took her a moment to realize he was leaning over her. "Sorry," she whispered in a voice he could scarcely hear. "You ought to do something about the trees around here. They keep falling over."

"Be quiet," he said in a rough voice, as his hands moved over her body, checking for breaks, for disastrous damage. There was no way he could tell for certain, but he suspected she was more bruised and shaken than seriously hurt, but she could scarcely lie in the ditch for much longer. It was starting to fill with water.

There was no choice for it. He slid his arms under her and scooped her up, staggering a bit under the unexpected weight.

"Run ahead and open the back door of the Rover, Mrs. Marvel," he called out, shifting Katie's weight against his chest.

The housekeeper paused, seemingly oblivious to the rain. "Maybe we can get around the tree and go straight into town if you've got the four-wheel-drive," she said eagerly. "The girl needs to be looked after...."

"We're taking her home," O'Neal said grimly. "The weather's too bad to risk it."

"But..." Mrs. Marvel made the rare attempt to argue.

"We're taking her home."

Katie lay limp in his arms, her head against his chest. "Put your arms around my neck," he said harshly, starting up the hill. "Don't just lie there."

She did as she was told, and he regretted it. She held tight to him, her face pressed against his shoulder, and he could feel the heat of her, the solid warmth of bone and soft, yielding flesh, and he knew if he had any sense at all he'd do as Mrs. Marvel had suggested, risk life and limb to get her out of his life as quickly as possible.

And he knew he wasn't going to. He'd tried to get rid of her, and almost killed her in doing so. Storms didn't last forever up here; they only seemed to. The house was huge—with her at one end and himself at another, he might not even have to see her again.

But he would. He would see her and touch her. And he would kiss her, delivering slow, deep, wet kisses that would ride out the storm. And if she stayed too long, he would take her, and risk absolutely everything.

Mrs. Marvel was already sitting in the back seat of the Rover, her arms out to take Katie inside with her. He relinquished her reluctantly, slamming the door and moving around to the driver's side.

"No need to look so grim, sir," Mrs. Marvel said as he carefully turned the car on the muddy track. "She got a bump on her head, nothing worse. We'll get her taken care of, and as soon as we're sure the storm is over, my Willie will take her into town."

"You should have waited," he said, watching the road with necessary intensity.

"You wanted her gone, didn't you, sir? You were in a real hurry to have her out of the house. I thought I was following your wishes."

"I wanted her gone," he said. "I still want her gone. But not at the expense of risking lives."

"Don't you worry, sir," Mrs. Marvel said in her cozy voice. "It'll take a lot to kill the likes of me. They breed us strong in the north country. Look at my Willie."

O'Neal thought of her hulking son with a lack of affection. "Indeed," he murmured. He peered ahead through the dark mists that had washed over the headlands. There was no sign of whatever had led him on. "You didn't see anything, did you, Mrs. Marvel?"

"Anything, sir? Such as what?"

"Something in the wind. White, like a sheet of paper or cloth or..."

"You're as bad as the girl here," Mrs. Marvel said in her comfortable voice. "She kept seeing things flapping about in the trees, dipping in front of the car. Let out a scream that scared me half to death, she did, and of course there was nothing there. Seeing ghosts, are you?''

''Hardly.''

''Neither did she, I expect. She's a silly girl. Maybe she did happen to see some paper blowing in the wind. I haven't seen or heard anyone or anything,'' she said. ''But then, you know I'm a practical woman. I don't put much store in superstition and the like. If I can't see it, touch it, taste it or smell it, I don't believe in it.''

''And what if you're not sure?'' They were already back within the stone courtyard, driving past the deserted guest house and parking in the garage. ''What if you can't be certain?''

Mrs. Marvel's face was round and cheery in the grim shadows of the storm-swept morning and the darkened stall. ''I'm not a woman to be plagued with uncertainty, sir.''

He wouldn't let himself look at the pale figure of the woman who lay in her lap. ''No, Mrs. Marvel,'' he said faintly, ''I imagine you're not.'' She was a good woman, he thought. Loyal, unflinchingly honest and straightforward. He trusted her, when he thought he could never trust anyone again. ''You'll take good care of her, won't you?''

Mrs. Marvel smiled with motherly charm. ''I'll take perfect care of her, sir. Me and my Willie.''

And it had to be the chilliness of the morning rain that sent a shiver across O'Neal's back.

Chapter Five

She'd had better days, Katie Flynn decided. Better weeks, as a matter of fact. All because she had a child's wide-eyed delight in nature on a rampage. Dozens of times she'd had the chance to stay put in some safe environment, and instead she'd pressed onward, which had left her in her current sorry situation: without a car, a purse, money, identification, stranded in the middle of nowhere with a killer headache and a second-string version of Mr. Rochester glowering at her.

Of course, it hadn't been her choice to leave this morning. Had she been able to find any reasonable excuse at all, she would have stayed in the drafty old mansion, ghosts and all.

Her pet ghost had followed them as they'd driven into the storm. Mrs. Marvel had seen nothing, of course, and Katie'd wondered whether she was having hallucinations. She'd seen the pale figure a handful of times since yesterday afternoon, and she couldn't blame the first accident and the stress of almost tumbling into the sea on the apparition, any more than she could blame it for the blow on her head when the huge tree had come crashing down on the expensive car.

Her noble rescuer had vanished once more, leaving Mrs. Marvel to help her back into the house. By the time they reached the hallway, Katie was shivering, and Mrs. Marvel steered her toward the library where she'd first sought shelter the night before. The fire was blazing, the oil lamps were lit against the darkness of the storm-laden day, and the room was deserted.

"O'Neal's gone out," Mrs. Marvel said, "and this is the warmest room in the huge, drafty old house. You stay by the fire, and I'll bring you some dry clothes and a mug of coffee."

"But..."

"Not to worry, dearie. Willie's gone with him, and there won't be any prying eyes to bother you. They won't be back till mid-afternoon, maybe later."

It was hardly reassuring, but she didn't have much choice in the matter. She was soaked to the skin, her body ached almost as much as her head, and she needed solitude, warmth and comfort. The deserted library provided all three.

Mrs. Marvel's dowdy clothes hadn't improved with age, but Katie was beyond caring as she hurriedly dressed, unable to stop the feeling that she was being spied upon. It was hardly worth their effort, she thought wryly. She was no *Playboy* centerfold. Her body was rounded, curved, with pale skin and a depressing abundance of golden freckles across her arms and chest. Hardly the stuff for erotic fantasies. Assuming O'Neal even indulged in such weakness.

She glanced around her as she buttoned the sweater, looking up at the paintings high on the wall. They were portraits, very old, and she had no doubt they belonged to O'Neal's family. The resemblance was unmistakable. Particularly striking was a woman with dark hair and eyes, a gypsy-ish smile, and a familiar-looking ring on her slender hand. Katie peered more closely, recognizing it immediately, the sea green stone that matched O'Neal's stormy eyes, the beautiful gold setting.

"That's Fiona," O'Neal's voice came from behind her. "One of my ancestors."

He was lucky she didn't scream, Katie thought, taking a deep, calming breath. He had the nastiest habit of creeping up on people unannounced.

"That explains it, then," she said with deceptive calm.

"Explains what?" He'd stripped off his raincoat, but his long hair was thick with rain, and the austere, beautiful lines of his face were still damp.

"My dream last night. I must have seen that portrait and mixed it up in my head."

"What did you dream?"

She wasn't about to tell him. He already thought

she was a complete idiot; she didn't need to tell him she thought she'd seen a ghost. Besides, there was no more than a superficial resemblance between the ghost girl and the vibrant woman in the portrait. Different coloring, decades difference in age. They weren't the same—Katie must have seen the portrait, and her imagination had done the rest.

"Mrs. Marvel said you and Willie were out for the afternoon," she said instead, keeping the accusation out of her voice. She couldn't imagine him skulking around, peering at her out of the shadows, but she couldn't shake the feeling that someone had been watching her.

"I have no idea where Willie is—I'm hardly his keeper. And it's not a day for a pleasant country stroll. I came in five minutes ago." He glanced at the pile of soaked clothes on the stone hearth, then back at her. "And I didn't watch you undress, if that's what you're fussing about. It hardly seems worth the trouble."

"It wouldn't be," she said. "I'm certain you've seen thousands of women who are far more attractive than I am."

A very faint smile appeared on his face only to vanish just as quickly, and she wasn't sure if she found that amusement annoying or curiously flattering. "Not quite thousands," he said slowly. "How's your head doing?"

Funny, his entrance into the room had banished all thought of a headache from her consciousness.

"Not too bad," she said, brushing her damp hair away from her forehead. "It's just a bump."

"Mrs. Marvel tells me you think you saw a ghost," he said, taking the wing chair by the fire and stretching his legs out. He was wearing black jeans and a black shirt, and she never would have thought clothes like that could look both ridiculously elegant and absurdly sexy.

"Do I look like the kind of woman who believes in ghosts?"

"Yes."

She wasn't going to dignify that with a response. She moved closer to the fire, rubbing her arms briskly. "How long do you think the storm will last?"

He glanced toward the leaded-glass windows. "A few hours," he said. "A few days. Storms have a will of their own, and when they meet up with the sea then there's no telling what will happen. It's a waste of time trying to second-guess nature, or having a temper tantrum because things aren't going your way."

"I agree," she said sweetly. "So it looks like you're stuck with me for however long it takes."

He turned his gaze from the window, and his eyes were the color of the storm. He looked at her, a long, slow perusal that started at the top of her damp hair and ended up at her bare feet beneath Mrs. Marvel's voluminous skirts. "You make it sound as if I was trying to get rid of you."

"Aren't you?"

"Yes."

It was a conversation stopper, and Katie was tired of trying. The man was annoying, unsettling, and his eyes were doubtless the cause of her strange dreams. "I'll be gone as soon as it's safe to leave, and I promise to do my best to keep out of your way and your precious solitude."

"I don't know how precious it is," he said, half to himself. "But it's necessary."

"Why?"

"I do better cut off from people."

She looked at him in surprise. "Well, granted you're singularly lacking in social graces, that doesn't mean you couldn't be more pleasant if you tried."

"It's not my lack of social graces that worries me," O'Neal said in a mild voice.

"Then what is it? Do you turn into a werewolf at night and rip out strangers' throats?"

She was unprepared for his reaction. He looked startled, and then he laughed, full and loud. "You're closer than you could ever think. Lock your doors at night, Katie Flynn, and don't pay any attention to howling sounds or creatures clawing at your door."

"I don't believe in werewolves."

"Only ghosts," he said pleasantly. "Well, I don't believe in ghosts, but I believe in shape shifters."

"Shape shifters?" There was a rumble of thunder in the distance, like a bad old movie.

"Creatures who change their shape. Men who turn into wolves or bats or seals."

"Good God, next thing you'll be telling me you believe in vampires," she scoffed, ignoring the chill that danced across her backbone.

"You've never seen me in sunlight, have you?"

He was teasing her, but there was no affection in it. "I don't think the sun shines on the state of Maine."

"Certainly not in October."

"Are you telling me you're a vampire?"

He laughed, a faintly bitter sound. "No vampire, no werewolf, no ghost. No banshee wailing at your window. You have an overwrought imagination."

"And you're doing your best to make it jump through hoops." She took a sip of her coffee.

"Are you going to tell me about your ghost?" he persisted.

She glanced at him over the rim of the cup. "Why are you so interested?"

"If it's haunting my house I should think I have a right to be concerned. I'm wondering if this is an evil specter."

"I don't think so," she said. "It's a young girl."

He dropped his cup of coffee. It shattered on the stone floor, splashing his legs. He ignored it, staring at her, and his sea green eyes were strange, haunted.

"Describe her." He was obviously trying to sound casual, but the effort was beyond him.

"About fourteen or fifteen. Long, white-blond hair, green eyes."

"Is she unhappy?"

"Not particularly. I'd say she seems more determined, maybe a bit curious. I thought you didn't believe in ghosts?" she added sharply.

"I don't," he said, and she didn't believe him for a moment. "I'm humoring you."

If O'Neal didn't believe in ghosts he was acting very oddly indeed, even for him. "Kind of you," she said. "Her name's Fiona."

The color drained from his face. He no longer looked strange, he looked furious. He crossed the room, crushing the broken cup beneath his feet, and caught her arms in a hard grip. "All right," he said sharply, "who put you up to this? Someone in town? I can't believe Mrs. Marvel would be a party to something so cruel...."

"I don't know what you're talking about!" she protested. He wasn't hurting her, but he was much too close, his hands were too strong, and she wanted, needed to move away from him.

"'Her name's Fiona,'" he mimicked savagely. "What a strange coincidence. She told you that, did she? What else did she say? Did she happen to tell you why she'd suddenly decided to start haunting this place after fifteen years?"

"She didn't tell me anything. It was just a feeling

I had, a sense that that was her name,'' Katie said, bewildered. ''And what do you mean, after fifteen years? Who's Fiona?''

''My sister,'' he said bleakly, releasing her abruptly and turning away from her.

Katie didn't move, her bare feet frozen to the thick carpet. He had his back to her, and some utterly idiotic part of her wanted to go up and put her arms around him, to rest her head against his back and hold him. Comfort him.

But O'Neal didn't want her comfort. He didn't want her presence, her touch, her ghost stories or her reassurances. He wanted her gone, and it was the least she could do.

She started to leave, determined to give him his solitude. Unfortunately her feet were bare, the broken coffee cup lay directly in her path, and she was too busy trying to be circumspect to pay attention to where she was walking. She stepped full force on a shard of china.

She managed to bite off her yelp of pain, but not quickly enough. O'Neal whirled around with an impatient glare, and Katie immediately sat in the nearest chair, plastering an innocent expression on her face.

''What now?'' he demanded.

''Nothing.'' She was attempting to sound at ease, even as she felt the blood begin to drip from her foot, but she ended up sounding faintly hysterical. ''I just thought I'd sit here and—''

"And drip blood all over my carpet," O'Neal said wearily. "I think I preferred the rainwater."

So much for being subtle. She tried to rise, but he simply pushed her back into the chair, dragging a footstool over and planting himself upon it. "I'm fine," she said, as he took her bleeding foot into his lap. "I don't need…"

"Hold still and be quiet," he said, but his beautiful hands cradled her bare, bleeding foot with exquisite care. "I need to make sure you don't have any shards left."

"I doubt it. I'm sure Mrs. Marvel—ow!" She glared at him. "You did that on purpose."

"I'd rather you didn't leave a trail of blood all over the house, either," he said. "It doesn't look that serious. Are you always so accident prone?" He'd pulled a snowy white handkerchief from his pocket and began to fold it crosswise.

"Not usually," she said, looking askance at the makeshift bandage.

He must have noticed her expression. "Don't worry, it's clean," he said. "I wouldn't want a blood infection to lengthen your stay."

"I'm sure you wouldn't." She forced herself to sit back in the chair, watching his expert ministrations with a wary eye. His hands were cool against her skin, strong hands, smoothing the bandage around her foot. How would those hands feel against other parts?

Not that she was about to find out, or even

wished to. She had reached the advanced age of twenty-eight without ever succumbing to the lure of sex, and she wasn't about to start with a half-baked, brooding hero.

It hadn't been a conscious decision on her part, at least not until she'd reached her early twenties, the only virgin left at Mount Holyoke. She just hadn't been interested enough to sleep with her boyfriends. There were times when she wondered whether she was just plain sexless, but moments like these reassured her. She was healthy, normal, red-blooded. She was just waiting for the right man and the right time, neither of which had turned up yet.

It wasn't a matter of old-fashioned morality, or even common sense. Instinct told her that there was only one man for her, and when she found him she would know, and it would be forever. In the meantime she could enjoy her freedom.

But she looked at O'Neal's dark, beautiful face as he cradled her foot, and a strange, twisting ache began to form in the pit of her stomach.

"I'll have Mrs. Marvel see about getting you some lunch," he said abruptly, releasing her foot and moving away.

She felt oddly dizzy, but she wasn't going to let him see it. "Why?" she said. "I'm not particularly hungry."

"Aren't you? You were looking at me as if I were a piece of blueberry cheesecake."

If he'd mentioned any other kind of food she would have been all right. But why in the world would he pick the one food, the one secret vice she found irresistible? He didn't say strawberry cheesecake, or cannoli, or apple pie. He said blueberry cheesecake, as if he knew the depths of her soul.

"I don't like blueberry cheesecake." The lie came out of nowhere, an instinctive defense against God knew what.

The moment the words were out of her mouth a crack of thunder rattled the leaded-glass windows, and Katie jumped guiltily, as if caught by the Almighty in a falsehood. "Then I'll have her bring you some gruel," O'Neal said.

Katie rose to her feet, favoring the one tentatively. She wanted to get away from him, as fast she as she could. Her foot was tender, but not unbearably so.

"That's all right," she said. "I can look out for myself. I'll leave you in peace."

She half expected him to say something dour and dramatic. She half expected him to try to stop her, but this time he simply stood still and watched her limp to the door, carefully skirting the remnants of the broken coffee cup.

"Do you mind if I wander around a bit?" she asked.

A faint smile twisted his elegant mouth. "There are no hidden rooms or secret dungeons, Katie Flynn. Wander to your heart's content. I have no secrets in these stone walls. And no ghosts named Fiona, either.''

She didn't believe him. There were ghosts, and secrets that haunted him, and if she had any sense at all she'd grab a book and immure herself in her allotted bedroom and keep her foolish curiosity at bay.

But common sense was a highly overrated commodity, she always thought. Her unwilling host was a mystery, and Katie had never been able to resist a good mystery. Particularly when the alternative seemed to be dusty Victorian novelists.

"If you say so, O'Neal," she said politely enough. And she closed the door behind her with silent care.

THE KITCHEN was deserted—Mrs. Marvel was nowhere to be seen. There were a few fresh muffins still on top of the old kitchen range. Katie helped herself to one, then wandered over to the refrigerator in an unsuccessful search for diet Coke. Coffee was all well and good, but she needed carbonation and chemicals to feel human, and this house was sadly lacking in both. The power had come back on at some point, though the sparse electric lighting did little to dispel the gloom of the day.

"Mrs. Marvel?" she called out tentatively, suddenly lonely.

"She ain't here."

Katie fumbled her muffin, almost dropping it as

Willie loomed out of the shadows. He was absolutely huge—six and a half feet of bulk. He loomed over her, coming much too close, and she backed up nervously, unable to help herself. She was being foolish, shamefully so, and she knew it. The poor man couldn't help what he looked like, couldn't help the fact that his mental acuity wasn't all that it should be. In the electric light she could see a long, jagged scar across the top of his forehead, beneath his shaggy hair, and it gave him the eerie look of Frankenstein's monster. Perhaps he hadn't been born that way, after all, perhaps it had been an accident....

He touched her. He lifted his giant, hamlike hand and stroked her hair, and it was all she could do not to shudder. It wasn't gentle simplicity she saw in his eyes. It was malice, clear and plain.

"Willie!" Mrs. Marvel's voice was sharp and full of warning. "Leave the girl alone."

Willie dropped his hand, lowering his eyes as he stepped away from her, and Katie realized she'd been holding her breath. "Yes, Ma. I didn't mean no harm."

"Of course you didn't, my boy. But you know what I've always told you about young ladies."

"Yes, ma'am," he muttered, shuffling away from her and taking a seat at the table.

Katie looked down at her hand. The muffin was crushed in her fist, and crumbs were falling on the floor at her bare feet. She looked down at the same time Mrs. Marvel did.

"Never you mind, my dear," she said in her soft, soothing voice. "A kitchen's made for spilled food. But what in heaven's name happened to your poor foot?"

"I stepped on some broken china. O'Neal dropped his coffee cup."

"How odd," Mrs. Marvel said. "O'Neal is never clumsy." She looked at her curiously. "You must have an unusual effect on him. But that's not to wonder at, such a pretty thing you are. Still and all, O'Neal's never shown any interest in the frailer sex."

Katie wasn't feeling particularly frail, and Mrs. Marvel scarcely fit that description, but she kept her opinion to herself. "I annoy him."

"Oh, I imagine you do," Mrs. Marvel said comfortably. She moved closer, blocking her son's vacant stare, and she smelled of vanilla and fresh coffee and starched laundry. "Let me give you a little hint of warning," she said in a lower voice. "The men in this house aren't quite…right. My Willie wouldn't harm a soul, but there are times when he doesn't know his own strength. As for O'Neal—there's no knowing. I've worked for him for more than twelve years and I know less about him than when I started. If I were you I'd keep to myself while the storm lasts and you're here with us. It's safer that way." She patted her lightly on the shoulder.

If Mrs. Marvel had meant to be reassuring she had failed miserably. Katie could feel a superstitious shiver run up her backbone, and it was only her fierce self-will that made her able to smile serenely.

"O'Neal said it would be all right if I explored a bit this afternoon," she said. "There isn't much else for me to do. Unless I could help you...."

"Heavens, no, dearie!" She laughed comfortably. "I'm more than capable of taking care of this old house. I'll see that Willie keeps his distance, and you can explore all you want. There's not much to see, mind you. Most of the rooms are closed off. Just a bunch of dust and old furniture."

"I'm just curious."

"Best be careful, Katie," she said sweetly. "You know what they say—curiosity killed the cat. You've already been a bit accident-prone, and this old house isn't the safest place in the world. Some of these rooms have been shut up for decades or more."

"I'll be fine. If I don't show up by dinnertime you can send out a search party," she said lightly.

Mrs. Marvel glanced back at her silent son. "I'll come find you myself," she said. "Safer that way."

And for some inexplicable reason, Katie shivered.

Chapter Six

As a child Katie had loved nothing more than to read. Losing herself in a book had always been her favorite form of recreation and escape, and she still never went anyplace without at least two things to read in her knapsack, just in case she finished the first book.

Unfortunately her stash of murder mysteries and romance novels were now being enjoyed by the fishes, and nothing on this earth would make her go back to the library where O'Neal reigned in gloomy majesty, all for the dubious reward of a Charles Dickens novel. Besides, the old stone house was like something out of a gothic novel. All she needed was a flowing white nightgown and a candlestick to fit the bill.

Of course, that was exactly what she'd had the night before, as she'd gone in search of the brooding master of the house and had almost gotten kissed. Well, in actual fact he had kissed her, but not on the mouth.

In the murky light provided by low-wattage light bulbs and stormy daylight, the room Mrs. Marvel had put her in looked distressingly barren. The only furniture remaining was the huge oversize bed, still piled high with quilts. The leaded-glass windows looked out over gray, storm-swept sea. The rain had slowed to a steady drizzle, lashing against the windows with monotonous regularity, and she peered up into the leaden sky, looking hopefully for a patch of light. There was none to be seen. For some reason the notion of a major hurricane was no longer nearly so enchanting.

There were no curtains at the windows, no paintings on the walls, no rugs to warm the chilly, slate floors. She pulled on a pair of heavy kneesocks and headed for the door, stopping long enough to peer at her reflection in the wavery mirror. She had a noticeable bump on her forehead—it was a wonder her head didn't hurt beyond a dull ache. Her flyaway red hair had dried once more from its recent soaking, but the constant dampness was doing little to help control its wild tendencies. It curled around her face in a torrent of waves.

She stared at her face for a moment, momentarily distracted. "You look different, Katie Flynn," she said out loud. "Maybe it's the ridiculous clothes, or the gloomy mansion, or one too many bumps on the head, but you don't look like yourself."

The pale, elfin creature in the mirror didn't reply, and Katie shook her head. "Remember who you are," she ordered herself. "You're a sensible woman, old enough to know better. Just because you have a tendency to be superstitious, gullible and romantic..." Her voice trailed off with a sudden choke. She wasn't alone in the mirror.

It had to be her overwrought imagination, of course. The mirror was ancient, the reflection distorted, and the light in the room untrustworthy to say the least. Outside, the wind howled like a hungry wolf, tree branches tapped against the windows, and inside, a pale, ghostly face stared out of the mirror beside Katie Flynn.

She didn't want to turn her head, to look over her shoulder and see if the apparition was truly there. If she did so it would be to admit that she believed, and if she believed then she was prey to...to everything. So she kept her face straight ahead, staring into the mirror, expecting to see the willowy wraith of Fiona.

But it was no flaxen-haired child staring at her with such fixed determination. Standing behind the shoulder of Katie Flynn, the reflection was a bearded, red-haired man of late middle age and genial temperament. She hadn't realized the ghosts were in color, she thought absently. Fiona was so pale she'd seemed almost invisible. The man in her mirror was pale, as well, as if a veil of gray stood between them, but there was still no mistaking the grizzled red of his hair, or even the bright rosiness of his cheeks.

He leaned closer to her reflection, close enough to whisper in Katie's ear, but she could feel no one behind her. The ghost was in the mirror and nowhere else. She stood, transfixed, watching as the man whispered in her reflection's ear.

"Watch yourself, Katie dear." The voice was thickly Irish, directly in her ear, and she whirled around, the spell broken, ready to confront the trickster who'd crept up behind her.

There was no one there. She turned back to the mirror, but he was gone there, as well, only the wavering reflection of her own troubled face staring back at her.

And the oddest thing of all was that she wasn't frightened. Confused, perhaps. Disturbed. But not frightened. Whoever had materialized in the mirror and whispered in her ear, he meant her no harm.

The absurdity of the situation suddenly struck her, and she whirled away from the mirror. Believing in ghosts and superstitions was one thing, actually seeing and hearing them was another. Maybe she'd hit her head harder than she thought. Maybe she was living in some old "Twilight Zone" episode. Maybe her car had really gone over the cliff and she was now suspended in some strange world between life and death.

Or maybe she was simply letting an always gullible imagination get out of hand. She reached for the doorknob, ready to step into the hallway, when at the last minute she spun around and peered into the mirror once more. There was nothing in the silvery reflection but a troubled young woman.

"Well," she said in a practical voice, "at least it isn't vampires. They wouldn't show up in a mirror." And on that note of dubious comfort she started her explorations.

There was no doubt about it—the majority of the old house was barren indeed. She'd been hoping for something out of *A Secret Garden*—hidden rooms and miniature ivory elephants. Instead she found what looked like cells, small rooms carved out of larger ones, with barred windows, narrow iron beds and dusty tables. It didn't look as if anyone had set foot in them for decades, and an air of melancholy clung to the place, like the cries of lost souls.

But there were no ghosts. In those rooms where tormented people had once lived, the air was still and empty. No wandering spirit haunted the rooms, looking for ease. If the huge old mansion were truly haunted, it wasn't by the former inmates. Both Fiona and the old man had seemed far too cheerful.

Unless, of course, Katie Flynn was the one going mad.

She didn't really think it likely. Mental health was one thing her family had always had in annoying abundance. Katie herself had ruled out life as an artist early on. Much as she loved to paint— loved the sensuous wash of colors on a canvas, the smooth pleasure of a brush in her hand—she simply wasn't neurotic enough or impractical enough to choose such an unlikely calling. Though if she spent long enough at this house even she might turn a bit odd.

She left the cells behind, happily enough. There were other, larger bedrooms, just as barren, and beyond the dusty, streaked windowpanes she could see the day growing darker as the storm drew down on them again. Each of the rooms had been stripped of anything of value—no books, paintings and, thankfully, no mirrors were left. Only haphazard, broken furniture. Except for one bedroom.

The moment she opened the door she knew she should withdraw, immediately. It could only be O'Neal's bedroom, and she had no business nosing around it.

It was also the only interesting place she'd come across so far, and clearly O'Neal was nowhere around, or he would have ordered her from the place quite loudly.

"Go ahead, Katie." The male voice came from nowhere on the breath of a sigh, and this time she knew she wasn't talking to herself. "Watch your back," that same voice had warned her, and she found she trusted him.

She stepped inside O'Neal's room and closed the door behind her. At one end of the room a row of glass doors led out onto a stone parapet, and the light that filtered through them was murky, giving the large room an almost underwater look. The bed was huge, ornate, hung with green damask hangings, the floor was tiled with a mosaic pattern that almost looked Roman. The marble fireplace still held the remnants of a fire, and the room was still warm despite the howl of wind, the lash of the rain against the glass doors.

She walked over to them, peering out into the raging afternoon, at the wide parapet beyond the doors. On a clear, sunny day, the balcony that looked out over the ocean would probably be a lovely place to sit and read. Right now it brought the angry ocean almost to the door.

She turned to look back at the huge old bed. It reminded her of a room she'd seen in the Metropolitan Museum in New York, years ago. The green and gold bedroom from a Venetian palazzo had seemed suspended in light and water, just as this room did. There was a multibranched candelabra at the head of the bed and haphazard piles of books. She picked one up and found herself smiling. It was the latest *Star Trek* novel. Who would have thought it of the dour O'Neal?

"I must say, I approve." There was that voice again, the rough, whiskey-tinged Irish voice. She looked around her, but there was no sign of anyone, no sign of a mirror. "Women are too skinny nowadays." The voice went on to say. "I like a woman with meat on her bones. Glad I am that the lad is finally showing some taste."

The room was empty...and warm—so much for

the notion that ghosts brought an icy chill when they appeared. Not that this particular ghost had made another appearance. Only the faintly lascivious voice echoing in her head.

"Who are you?" Her voice sounded unnaturally loud in the stillness.

There was no answer, of course. Ghosts didn't seem to relish direct questions. The storm was increasing in intensity, battering against the glass doors and shaking them with the force of the wind. And then the voice came again, from the rain-lashed parapet. "You can call me Da if you've a mind to."

There was a sudden flash of lightning, followed almost immediately by an earth-shaking clap of thunder, and beyond the glass panes she saw him again, untouched by the weather, grinning back at her like an oversize leprechaun.

She leaped for the door, pushing it open, but of course there was no one out there. Only the fierce storm that immediately soaked her, the wind that battled her for possession of the glass door.

She fought, desperately trying to drag the door closed again, but the storm had a mind of its own, and her own strength was surprisingly puny against the fierceness of the wind. It was all she could do to keep hold of the door, to keep it from smashing against the outer stone wall, when a strong hand reached out of nowhere, covered hers as she clung to the handle and pulled the door shut, pulling her safely inside the relative haven of O'Neal's bedroom.

She leaned against the door, panting, rain soaked, loath to look at her rescuer. She should have known it would be O'Neal. At least he was preferable to the leering Willie.

"Oh, it's you," she said with a singular lack of cleverness.

He shoved his hair away from his rain-damp face. "And who were you thinking it was?" he said sharply. "Everyone else in this house has the sense to grant me some privacy."

"Well, you could have been the ghost," she said brightly.

"I'm a little bigger than a teenage girl, aren't I?"

"No, I thought you were the other one."

He just looked at her. She was going from the frying pan into the fire, she thought dismally. It was bad enough that she was caught snooping around his bedroom, it was even worse when she started prattling about ghosts and such. "Another ghost?" he said with cool disbelief. "What is it this time? An Elizabethan lady with her head tucked underneath her arm?"

"An old man," she blurted out. "Well, maybe closer to middle age than old. I thought he was out on the parapet, but when I opened the door he wasn't there."

"I've lived here for fifteen years and I've yet to see a ghost."

"That's because you don't want to."

"And you do?"

"Well, not precisely...."

"And you've got it wrong. There's nothing I'd like to see more than my sister Fiona again. But ghosts aren't real, Katie Flynn. They only appear to hysterical women desperate for attention."

He really did bring out the absolute worst of her red-haired temper. She made it a moral tenet never to hit anyone, never to lash out physically in anger, but the supercilious, far-too-beautiful O'Neal was eroding those principles rapidly.

"It's not my fault if teenage girls and dirty old men decide to visit me," she said, mustering her dignity. "I must simply be more sensitive than you are. Which should come as no surprise, given your consistently rude behavior."

"You're thinking I'm insensitive?"

"I think you're a pigheaded boor," she said recklessly.

"And I think you're a prying, neurotic, hormonal chatterbox without the least sense of delicacy."

"You told me I could explore!" she snapped.

"I didn't expect you to make yourself at home in my bedroom and then start making up more ghosts to give yourself an excuse for being where you shouldn't be."

She was so mad she couldn't speak, so she simply glared up at him in impotent fury.

"You see," he added with a fatal tinge of smugness, "you can't even come up with a suitable excuse."

She hit him. It was a shameful rupture of her Irish temper, and she knew she should be sickened instead of gleeful as her fist barreled into his stomach. He let out a whoosh of pain, doubling over, and with difficulty she resisted the impulse to hit him again.

"Good for you, lass. He's more than deserving." The voice crowed in her ear.

"Shut up, Da," she muttered underneath her breath.

O'Neal jerked his head up, staring at her in the murky, watery light. Odd that those clear green eyes would still be beautiful when they were looking frankly murderous.

"What did you call me?" There was no mistaking the fury in his voice.

"I wasn't talking to you," she said. Repentance was beginning to set in. "I'm sorry I hit you, but you can be so annoying...."

He ignored her apology. "If you weren't talking to me then who were you talking to?"

She sighed. She supposed she couldn't blame him for not believing her, but at times the man was so *thick*. "The ghost," she said patiently. "The second one."

He stared at her for a moment. "There are any number of nice safe rooms we can put you in," he said finally. "You'll be well taken care of, until we can get you to a doctor."

"I'm not crazy."

"There are no ghosts, Katie."

"Then why have I seen two already?"

"Why stop at two? Maybe a whole bunch of them will march in and have a party. You can play bridge with them, or gossip about me."

"Trust me, you're not that interesting," she drawled, quite proud of herself. It was a complete and total lie. They both knew it, but she still managed to sound wonderfully blasé.

"Go away," he growled. "Go back to your room and leave me in peace. If there are any ghosts around the place they certainly aren't hanging out in my room."

"Actually the old man was watching from the balcony," she told him with more honesty than tact. "That's why I opened the door...."

"Go away," he said again, his voice dangerous.

Katie went.

THERE WERE NO LOCKS on the doors of the upper rooms of the old house—O'Neal had never had any reason to lock anyone out. The only people who had ever stayed there were Mrs. Marvel and her son, and they kept to their own quarters. Besides, he had no secrets, no priceless possessions that he had to protect with lock and key. Whatever treasures he found he could replace easily enough.

He had secrets, of course, but no one was going to discover them, not unless they stood out on the cliffs and watched as he dove into the icy water. Even then they'd be unlikely to see anything, or if they did, they wouldn't believe their eyes. His secret was safe, simply because it was so absurd.

And his priceless possessions meant little to him. Booty he'd rescued off the ocean floor, archaeological treasures, Spanish doubloons, gold and silver and fine gems. He no longer bothered to retrieve them when he came across them, and those he had lay piled in a dark storeroom. If he occasionally had need of ready cash he would find something and send it off to a New York dealer who handled such things for him, no questions asked. Not that there was any question about the authenticity or the legality of the booty. The danger lay in people who insisted on knowing who had recovered such treasures, and how.

But the unexpected, unwanted arrival of Katie Flynn had changed everything. He'd been a fool to tell her she could explore—next thing he knew he'd find her down in the storeroom, bedecked in Spanish Conquistador gold and black pearls from the Orient.

He'd have Willie put a bolt on his bedroom door, something that Miss Nosy couldn't get past. Either that or he'd make sure Katie was never out of sight of one of his servants.

It was a logical alternative, but he couldn't be

comfortable with the notion. Willie was harmless, always had been. There was no reason for O'Neal to feel uneasy at the thought of Willie watching Katie Flynn.

Reason or not, he didn't like it. No more than he liked finding her in his bedroom. He'd think of her tonight when he went to bed, remember her in his room, the look of her, the scent of her.

He'd think of her, anyway, whether she'd been there or not, and he knew it. He was getting almost as crazy as she was. He didn't know whether she actually imagined she saw ghosts, or simply wished she did. Either way, she wasn't making her unwanted presence any easier to tolerate.

He walked back to the glass door, staring out over the rain-lashed parapet. He could see the ocean beyond Seal Point, churning and thrashing with wild abandon. The storm was worsening and it would be unlike anything he had ever seen. He knew it in his bones, in his flesh, in his hide. There would be no escape for any of them before it hit, not for Katie Flynn or the Marvels or, God help him, O'Neal. They would be trapped there, at the mercy of the weather. And only one of the four had the wherewithal to survive.

He narrowed his eyes, looking for something, anything, that the foolish creature might have mistaken for a ghost. There was nothing, of course, and hadn't been for fifteen years. If there were ghosts haunting the old house, then they would have found him long ago. He'd been waiting for them.

He pushed the door open, letting the rain and wind beat down on him. The fierceness of the downpour made him blink, but he didn't move, staring into the dark afternoon with stubborn intensity.

"Da?" he said softly, but the wind caught his voice and whipped it away to the heavens. There was no sign of his father out there in the raging storm. No red-haired old man with too strong a fondness for young ladies and Irish whiskey and tall tales.

No teenage sister watching over him. They were in their graves, along with his mother, and had been since that terrible night more than fifteen years ago, when his family had drowned, and he had found out just who and what he was.

He slammed the door shut again, and one of the panes of glass cracked with the force of it. He'd found some dubious sort of peace, until Katie Flynn had come, stirring things up with her talk of Da and Fiona.

But peace would come again. The storm would pass, sooner or later, and Katie Flynn would leave. And O'Neal would be alone and safe once more, secure in his solitude.

In the meantime, if things got too bad, he could always take to the sea.

"Now, then, Willie, what are you doing down there?" Mrs. Marvel called out to her son at the bottom of the dank cellar stairs.

"Nothin', ma," he called back dutifully.

Mrs. Marvel raised her flashlight high, peering down the stone steps into the darkness. "I won't have you keeping secrets from me, Willie," she warned. "You don't like it when I have to punish you."

Willie's shaggy head appeared at he foot of the stairs. "I'm getting ready, Ma. You told me you wanted me to take care of the girl, didn't you?"

Mrs. Marvel paused. "I was planning on a simple accident. It would be much safer if she just broke her neck falling. The steps are treacherous in this old house, and the lights are forever going out. It wouldn't take much for her to tumble to her death, and fewer questions asked."

"But you promised me, ma," he said plaintively.

"But, Willie, we don't want to have to answer questions, now, do we?"

"A couple of days in the sea and they won't know what happened to her in the first place," Willie said confidently. "If they even find her. It's just as easy to tumble over a cliff as it is down a flight of stairs."

Mrs. Marvel smiled at her offspring fondly. "My boy, there are times when it seems you might not be as stupid as I thought you were. But we have to remember, it's the money we're after. That's what we've worked so hard for all these years. We must never lose sight of that.''

Willie ducked his head in embarrassed pleasure at the praise. ''I know, Ma. But what about him?'' he said. ''How long do we have to wait?''

Mrs. Marvel glanced back into the dimly lit kitchen. The tray of tea sat untouched on the kitchen table—when she'd gone to take it to O'Neal he was nowhere to be seen.

''Maybe the sea will take care of him, as well,'' she said. ''We should be so lucky.''

''How much longer?'' Willie's voice was a soft whine.

She could hear the wind howling outside. ''It's a fierce storm, Willie,'' she mused. ''Bigger than any we've had in years. I think O'Neal and his young friend aren't going to survive this hurricane. It will be a sad, sad thing, but what can you expect when you live so far out, away from civilization?''

Willie frowned, confused. ''You mean we have to wait and see if the storm kills him, ma?''

''No, dear,'' she said sweetly. ''We'll kill him ourselves. Soon, dearest. Very soon.''

Chapter Seven

Katie had gone straight back to her room, crawled into bed and pulled the covers over her head, still fuming about the impossible O'Neal. Punching her soft, feather pillow wasn't nearly as satisfying as punching O'Neal's flat stomach, but at least she didn't need to feel guilty about letting her temper get out of hand. As long as she kept her rage in the confines of her room she'd be just fine.

"Ghosts," she muttered to herself. "He's right, I am crazy."

"You're not, darlin'," came the voice. "Don't let him bamboozle you."

"Be quiet!" Katie snapped out loud, closing her eyes determinedly. The raucous ghost obeyed.

When she woke the air was curiously quiet. It was late afternoon, but the constant downpour seemed to have stopped, though Katie had little hope it was a permanent break in the weather. The light was strange—an eerie bluish calm spreading out over the angry ocean. Even the wind had stilled—there were no tree branches scraping at her window, no ghostly debris flapping past in the breeze.

She could see the cliff quite clearly for the first time since she'd arrived. The house was sitting out on a narrow spit of land, with the ocean all around, and the windswept coastline looked fierce and rocky.

There was no telling whether the storm was truly at an end or was merely taking a rest. Katie hadn't heard a weather report since she'd left the hotel yesterday morning, and back then no one had been certain of how extensive Hurricane Margo would be—whether it would hit the mainland at all or simply blow out to sea. For all Katie knew, it could have been downgraded to a tropical storm and be in the midst of petering out. Somehow she didn't think so.

There were no radios in the house, but there might be one in the Range Rover. She needed some kind of information, some sense of how long she was going to be trapped here. With any luck she'd find the hurricane had run its course and she'd be free to go. With any luck. It didn't matter that some strange, irrational part of her wanted to stay. She was used to resisting self-destructive and dangerous impulses.

There was no one in sight when she reached the kitchen—Mrs. Marvel and her hulking son must have been busy elsewhere. She found an oversize pair of rubber boots and shoved her feet into them, grabbed an old raincoat from the peg beside the door, and headed out into the hallway leading to the yard, half expecting someone to stop her.

The vehicles were kept in an old stable to the right of the building. At some point Willie must have fetched the Volvo—it stood in one bay, its hood crushed, windshield smashed, fender bent sideways. The Range Rover sat next to it, but there was no sign of anyone around. Katie cast a nervous glance over her shoulder. If Willie were to be anywhere close, the garage seemed a likely spot, but the place seemed thankfully deserted.

There was no key in the ignition of the Range Rover, and the radio didn't work without it. The Volvo was a different matter. Since the bashed-in vehicle was scarcely drivable, the key still hung in the ignition, and Katie slid behind the wheel, turned it, and flicked on the radio, desperate for any word of the outside world.

All she got for her trouble was static, the same crackling noise she'd gotten on her own car radio. The place must be in some strange sort of atmospheric hollow, she thought, searching vainly for any kind of clear reception. There was nothing, only a loud, buzzing noise.

She climbed back out of the car, taking another look at the damage with the vain hope that it might be drivable after all. Both front tires were flat, and one wheel was bent and twisted. If she were going to get out of here, back to civilization, the Volvo wasn't going to be the way to get her there.

She glanced out toward the deceptively still, late-afternoon air. There was always the possibility that she could walk for help. Right now, with the wind only an intermittent problem and the skies temporarily free from rain, walking looked like a perfectly reasonable alternative to being stuck in a chilly mausoleum with a man who obviously wanted her elsewhere.

But reason didn't seem to have anything to do with the ghosts who kept cropping up at various intervals. At least they weren't particularly frightening. They surprised her more than anything else.

The sky was beginning to grow darker again, and faint drops of rain came spitting from the sky. Katie peered out into the gathering gloom. She ought to go inside, find herself a cup of coffee and something non-Dickensian to read, and settle in for the evening. With luck she could eat in the cozy safety of the kitchen, instead of having O'Neal glower at her. Of course, Willie would be in the kitchen, as well, and Katie wasn't sure who she found more unsettling, the brooding master of this gothic mansion or his faintly sinister servant.

She ought to be ashamed of herself, she thought. There was absolutely nothing sinister about Willie Marvel. It was hardly his fault he was as he was. If it weren't for his strength she would have fallen into the sea, trapped in her Subaru, before O'Neal had a chance to drag her out.

She gave herself a little shake. Crazy or not, she was more frightened of harmless Willie Marvel than a bevy of ghostly apparitions, and no amount of sensible rationalizations could change her mind.

She glanced out over the steep cliffs, taking stock of her surroundings with a fresh eye.

It wasn't nearly as gloomy a place as it had seemed beneath the incessant rain. To be sure, the old stone mansion was like something out of a thirties' horror movie, but the land surrounding the place was stark and beautiful. Back on the mainland she could see the shuttered building that Mrs. Marvel had referred to as the guest house. Even though it was quite large, it was dwarfed by the old mansion that housed O'Neal and his servants, and it was much more appealing, with its weathered gray shingles, its haphazard porches, its rambling lines and shuttered windows.

Really, if O'Neal had any sense at all he'd move out of that mausoleum and into the smaller house, get himself some more reliable electricity, a cellular phone and maybe one of those minisatellite dishes so he could watch TV. It wouldn't go very well with his brooding-master-of-the-house moods, but Katie was growing rapidly tired of them, anyway, and if she was forced to stay here much longer she had every intention of telling him so the next time she saw him.

And then he'd probably throw her over the cliff, she thought with a faint grin. She set out across the muddy drive in the direction of the guest house. There must be a reason why it was deserted when the far less practical mansion housed its tiny population. Maybe the place was just too homey and cheerful for the likes of O'Neal. If she squinted she could almost imagine a serene Irish housewife standing on one of the upper porches, looking down over the sea with her practical arms crossed over her sturdy bosom.

Katie stopped and blinked. The late afternoon was clear and still—there were no scudding clouds, no bits of leaves or debris whipped in the air to cloud her vision. Granted, the light was strange, eerie, shadowed with the approaching twilight and the looming storm. But that was no shadow on the upper porch, staring down at her. It was a woman.

"Hey!" she called out. "Hey, you." It lacked imagination or any particular courtesy, but it was the only way Katie could think to get her attention.

It didn't work. The woman kept looking out to the sea, and as Katie drew closer she could see her face more clearly, the beautiful care-worn lines of a woman aging gracefully, the gentle mouth, the troubled eyes.

A gust of wind picked up, swirling past Katie, tossing her hair into her eyes and moving on toward the house. She shoved her hair back, opening her mouth to call out again, when she realized that the woman was unaffected by the wind. Her hair didn't move, her clothes didn't ruffle.

And then she turned to Katie, and their eyes met. Ghost eyes, full and sad. She turned again to watch the cliffs, the roiling ocean, and Katie followed her gaze, looking for something.

"Help him," the women said, her Irish voice echoing inside Katie's head. "You're the only one who can."

And then she simply vanished.

Ooooo-kay, Katie thought, letting out her breath with a whoosh of air. Clearly her imagination had gone completely haywire. O'Neal had suggested she play bridge with her ghosts. So far it seemed there were three of them—just the right amount for a foursome. Even if Da looked like the kind of man who would cheat.

In the distance she could hear a faint rumble of thunder, as if the fates were warning her she wasn't about to escape, not yet, at least. The temperature was dropping rapidly, and she huddled in the over-size raincoat, shivering. The notion of taking a casual stroll down to the edge of the cliff and trying to see what the ghost had been staring at was both unappealing and irresistible. Not that there were any such things as ghosts. She looked back at the guest house, but there was no sign of anyone on the upper porch. No ghost voices whispering in her ear.

The wind was growing strong, and she could feel the occasional spit of rain against her face. She ought to go back inside, immure herself again in that living tomb, before the storm picked up, but she was loath to do so. She wanted to enjoy the fresh air for as long as she could. And she wanted to see what the ghost woman had been staring at.

There were no such things as ghosts, she reminded herself doggedly as she headed for the cliffs. The wind was growing stronger now, and the trees were bending beneath its force. The rain had picked up, but the cold lash of it was refreshing against her skin. The sea called to her, the storm tide raging. But Katie loved the sea and the storm and the fierce winds whipping through her hair.

She wasn't sure what she expected to see in the churning water. The remnants of her rental car, perhaps, or a ghostly creature calling for her. For a moment she could see nothing but the waves crashing against the rocks, and then she narrowed her eyes against the sting of rain.

The seal was there again, riding easily on the storm-tossed water, staring up at her fixedly out of his dark eyes. The same seal she'd seen yesterday, she knew that without question, just as she knew it was a male. And that it recognized her.

She couldn't move. Even as the storm built around her once more, the rain pelted down, drenching her, she stood motionless at the edge of the cliff, staring into the lost eyes of the sleek brown seal. He was calling to her, she knew it. He wanted her to come to him.

You're the only one who can save him, the voice had told her, and in her mind Katie had thought of O'Neal, with his lost soul. But now it was the seal calling to her, floating in the water, riding the waves, waiting for her.

She took a step toward the edge of the cliff, without realizing what she was doing. Then another, the ground wet and crumbling beneath her feet, and she moved nearer to him.

The sound that came to her was strange, harsh, sudden. A deep, barking noise from the throat of the seal, warning her, sending her away. She fell back abruptly, then shook her head in belated panic. She'd been mesmerized by the churning water, the liquid eyes of the seal, and she'd been ready to take one more step, one that would send her plunging downward to certain death.

She took a deep, shaky breath. The seal had disappeared. His warning given, he'd dived into the black waves and vanished, and she was alone in the rain, trembling.

"YOU LOOK LIKE a drowned rat, dearie," Mrs. Marvel greeted her from her spot by the stove. "Take off those wet things and I'll give you a nice cup of tea. What in heaven's name made you wander out in such weather?"

Katie slipped into a chair near the stove. The normally cozy room felt cold and unwelcoming, but there was nowhere else she could go. "It had cleared for a while," she said. "I thought the storm might be ending."

Mrs. Marvel shook her head darkly. "Never trust the weather in these parts, Katie. Changeable as a woman, they say."

"Who says a woman is changeable?" Katie argued. "I tend to be remarkably steadfast."

Mrs. Marvel set a cup of steaming tea in front of her. It smelled of chamomile and mint, and Katie breathed in the scent with greedy pleasure. "Steadfast?" Mrs. Marvel echoed. "Or stubborn?"

"A bit of both, I suppose," she said with a sigh. "I know my faults too well."

"Well, there's nothing wrong with knowing your own mind." Mrs. Marvel sat down at the table beside her, and her usually cheery face was somber. "Dearie, we'll get you out of this place as soon as we can, I promise you that. In the meantime, the less you wander, the better. The cliffs are dangerous, the house itself is so huge there's no way Willie and I can keep up with it, and there are sections that are in poor repair. Dry rot and such. I'd hate to think of you breaking your neck in this old place."

"The notion doesn't appeal to me, either," Katie said lightly.

"And there are other things," Mrs. Marvel continued. "I worry about you, my girl. The best thing for it would be to get you safely out of here, but until we can, I think you ought to stay in your room.

I'll tell O'Neal you're not feeling well if he happens to want your company. Not that I think that's at all likely—he's a man who treasures his solitude, and your presence here disturbs him.''

Katie supposed she should have found the notion threatening. O'Neal wasn't the sort of man one would like to disturb. Nevertheless, a faint glow of pleasure warmed her.

"It's dangerous here, Katie Flynn." Mrs. Marvel's voice was low and doleful. "Keep out of his way, and you should be fine."

For a moment Katie didn't move. "Are you saying O'Neal would hurt me?" she questioned bluntly.

"I'm not saying anything. I'm just saying be careful." Mrs. Marvel rose, effectively putting an end to the conversation.

Katie wasn't so easily dismissed. "But…"

"I'll be bringing you your dinner tonight," Mrs. Marvel said brusquely, returning to the stove. "In the meantime, why don't you go and lie down? That was quite some bump on your head you got this morning. You might even have a slight concussion. You go rest, dearie. If you like, I'll have Willie see you to your room."

"No!" she said with unflattering haste. "I'll be fine." She was absolutely starving—it had been a long time since breakfast and no one apparently ate lunch around here. Her head was hurting, the rain had soaked through into her clothing, and her nerves were stretched taut.

"That's a good girl." Mrs. Marvel dismissed her, and Katie had no choice but to rise, as well.

She paused by the door to the hallway. "You've warned me about the house, the storm and O'Neal," she said. "What about the ghosts? Are they a danger as well?"

Mrs. Marvel turned to her, a wondering look on her face. "There are no such things as ghosts, Katie. Me and my Willie have lived here twelve years and never seen anything that doesn't have a rational, reasonable explanation. There are no ghosts, dearie."

Katie didn't move. She would have said the same thing twenty-four hours ago. Now she found herself accepting their existence as easily as she accepted her Catholic God.

"Maybe they only appear to me," she suggested.

"And why would that be?" Mrs. Marvel said with loving practicality. "Go lie down and rest your poor head, Katie dear. You've had a wild day and you know it."

It made no sense at all, Katie thought, loath to leave Mrs. Marvel's bracingly practical company. The next thing she knew, she'd start believing in shape shifters and zombies and man-eating aliens from outer space.

Maybe she was imagining them all. Actually there was no *maybe* about it. Superstitions were one thing, the supernatural was another entirely. "You're right," she said. She managed a smile. "I'm very lucky you were here, as well."

And Mrs. Marvel's answering smile was warm and benevolent.

HE WAS STANDING in the hallway, waiting for her.

Katie clamped her hands over her mouth to muffle her instinctive scream. O'Neal had loomed up out of nowhere, a shadowy, watchful figure, and in the gloom of the dimly lit hallway he unnerved her completely.

Of course, he would probably unnerve her on a bright sunny day, as well, she reminded herself with stern practicality. She looked up into his sea-colored eyes. "You scared the life out of me," she said breathlessly.

"Not quite." His clothes were dry, but his hair was wet and slicked back, and water still clung to his skin. He must have just come from the shower, and yet he smelled of the sea. A wild, erotic scent that seemed to reach out and catch her.

"What were you doing wandering down by the cliffs?" he continued in his cool, abrupt voice.

"And I always thought the Irish were so charming."

"Don't try to weasel out of it," he said sternly. "You could have fallen to your death. What in God's name made you decide to continue your wanderings out that way?"

"I was looking at the seal."

He took a deep breath, and it sounded oddly shaky in the stillness of the stone hallway. "Seals are a dime a dozen in these parts. If you're that interested in wildlife go to the zoo."

"I've only seen one seal here," she said. "Though I've seen him several times."

"How do you know it's the same seal? For that matter, how do you know it's a he?" O'Neal demanded.

"I just know. For one thing, he watches me."

O'Neal's laugh was without humor. "You think the seal's in love with you? What next, Katie Flynn? Two ghosts, an enamored seal and..."

"Three ghosts."

"Mary, Mother of God," he muttered, a prayer, not a blasphemy.

"Not her," Katie said.

O'Neal looked at her, and for a brief moment she thought she saw a glimmering of amusement in his bleak green eyes. It was gone before she could be certain. "God must have sent you here to torment me for my sins," he said with a sigh. "Next you'll be reading my palm and holding séances."

"No. I don't believe in those things."

"Only in ghosts?"

"And a seal who watches me," she added. His hair was very dark when it was wet. Deep soft brown like the thick rich fur of a seal. She let out a stray shiver. She was chilled, and the icy cold of the hallway was seeping into her bones.

He shook his head in disbelief. "You're ridiculous, you know that?" He sighed. "You're also cold. There's a fire in the library. You may as well come and warm up."

"How charming," she said, the ice in her voice as well as her damp body. "But I was just going back to my room."

"It'll be like a refrigerator there," he replied.

"I need another nap...."

"No, you don't. You've been sleeping too much as it is. With a head injury you need to stay awake and alert," he said sharply. "Come along to the library and I'll have Mrs. Marvel bring hot coffee and sandwiches."

She could resist the twin lures of a warm room and his unsettling presence, but the promise of food could seduce her at any time. She wavered, and he must have sensed it.

"The library has a grand view of the ocean," he said. "Maybe you can show me your passionate seal."

"I never said he was passionate, or enamored, or...anything. I just said he watches me."

"A stalker, is it?"

"You're annoying, aren't you?" she said with a weary sigh.

His response was a faint smile, one that reached his eyes and curved his beautiful mouth. One that transformed him from a fascinatingly beautiful man to a god. "It's what I do," he said sweetly.

She was so bemused by the sudden glory of that smile that she didn't resist when he took her arm in his. "Come along, Katie Flynn. I promise I won't eat you."

And Katie went.

Chapter Eight

He was a fool and a half to have brought her with
him. The less he was around Katie Flynn the better
off he was. She drew him, like a moth to a flame,
and yet flames were no part of a great deal of his
life. He wasn't worried about getting burned. He
was worried about drowning in her fire.

He found himself wondering how easy she was
as he watched her settle into one of the high-backed
chairs by the fire, tucking a throw around her.
Whether she was used to going off with mysterious,
possibly dangerous men. Perhaps he was wrong in
being so wary of her. Maybe he could simply take
her to bed, enjoy a few hours of mutual pleasure
until the storm passed and then send her on her way
with no regrets, recriminations or horror scenes.

It had been so long since he'd had a woman.

But Katie Flynn wasn't the one to break his celibacy, no matter how much she tempted him. Showing up on his doorstep like a drowned rat, she'd
upended his solitude, his hard-earned peace, his

very life, with her presence. Sleeping with her would only make things worse.

"Okay, I'm here," she said with a slightly pugnacious tilt to her chin. "Why did you want me?"

He could think of a million reasons. The tangled mane of red hair, the pale, luscious skin, the soft mouth that spoke too sharply, the blue eyes that saw too clearly. He wondered what would happen if he flirted with her, oh so gently? He'd probably lost the ability to flirt. It had been fifteen years since he'd last chatted up a pretty lady, not since the boating accident that had taken his family and ruined his life. Though his father would have insisted that a true Irishman never lost the ability to flirt.

"I want you to tell me about your ghosts," he said, leaning against the mantel and feeling the warmth of the fire sink into his bones. The ocean was so cold. "I've read all the books in the house and there's nothing else to do. Why don't you while away my time with ghost stories?"

She glanced around her, at the walls and walls of books that lined the library. "You've read all of the books?" she asked skeptically.

"All of them."

"I thought you didn't believe in ghosts. What are you trying to do, test the limits of my dementia?"

"Maybe I want to see if someone is playing a trick on you," he said, doing his best to keep from smiling. He wondered if Katie Flynn ever gave an inch. She reminded him of generations of strong

Irish women, tough and uncompromising and tender and loving.

"And who would that be? There are only the four of us here. Who do you think would be doing such mischief?"

"I trust the Marvels implicitly."

"There's no one else here," she said. "Unless you get your jollies staging apparitions. You know, I could well believe it of you. You don't want me here, and there's nothing you can do about it, so maybe you're getting revenge by scaring me to death."

"An interesting theory, but it has several holes. For one thing, these apparitions you keep seeing have the unfortunate effect of keeping you from leaving when I desperately want you to leave. For another, you don't seem the slightest bit frightened. Which makes me wonder whether you actually see anything at all? Any sensible woman would be terrified if she saw one ghost, much less two."

"Three," Katie corrected him glumly.

"Oh, yes, that's right. Three. Do you have the sight, Katie Flynn? Do you often see ghosts and banshees? Do you know things are going to happen before they do?"

"No."

He grimaced. "I expect not. If you knew the future you wouldn't have nearly driven off the cliffs."

"These are the first ghosts I've ever seen in my

twenty-eight years," she continued in a determinedly practical tone of voice, obviously hoping to lure him into thinking she was a sensible creature. "Maybe ghosts don't live in western Pennsylvania."

"Maybe they don't exist at all, either in Pennsylvania or Maine." He was warm enough now—the ocean chill had faded, and he sank down on the huge, shabby sofa with a weary sigh. "So why aren't you frightened of these ghosts?"

"Maybe because I know they don't mean me any harm."

"I thought one of them lured you to the cliffs. That sounds like malevolence to me. Your pet seal doesn't sound too helpful, either." He said it deliberately, waiting for her reaction. "Don't you believe in the existence of evil? Or are you one of those mindless, sunny creatures who think life is basically good?"

"I believe in evil," she said quietly. "I think there's evil here. I just don't think it comes from the seal or the ghosts. If anything, the ghost was trying to warn me away from the cliff."

"Who do you think it comes from, *macushla*? Me?"

A faint flush darkened her cheeks at the Irish endearment, even though it was spoken sarcastically. Maybe she knew as well as he did that the sarcasm was only a defense. And then she lifted her eyes and looked at him fully, and there was no fear in their utter blueness. "I don't know."

He wasn't sure what answer he had wanted from her. A declaration of trust would have been unwanted and unlikely. An avowal of dislike would have been the most practical solution. He wondered if she disliked him. He'd done everything he could to make it so.

"Why don't you ask one of your ghosts next time you see one?" he suggested with mock affability.

"I see them, I don't talk to them."

"But I thought they told you their names? Fiona and Da? Though both of those are pretty easy guesses. All Irish fathers are called Da, and Fiona's name is on the portrait over the mantel."

She looked up at the painting, giving him a chance to study her profile. Good bones, he thought. A stubborn chin, even as it dropped in shock, and she gasped.

"What's wrong?" he demanded, casting an irritated glance at the painting. It looked the same as always—the eyes hadn't come alive, no ghost emerged from the canvas. Lady Fiona Castlereagh O'Neal looked as stubborn, beautiful and sensible as she always had. She looked like his mother Maeve.

"The third ghost," Katie said in a hushed voice. "That's what she looks like. I saw her on the balcony at the guest house, staring out to sea, and I..."

He surged off the sofa, knocking the small table onto the floor. Coffee cups went flying, but he ignored them, stalking over to her with such fierceness that he could see the unwitting terror on her face. He leaned over her, his hands on the arms of the chair, trapping her there, and his anger was so strong he was beyond being sensible.

"I ought to break your neck," he said softly.

She stared up at him as if she had no idea what was bothering him. Lying, treacherous creature, with her smart mouth and her soft eyes. But she didn't cower, she simply met his gaze with stern courage. "Why are you trying to frighten me?" she asked.

He didn't back off. He had never deliberately hurt a woman in his life, and no matter what the temptation, he wasn't about to start now. He also didn't want her to realize that fact. He wanted her scared. "Someone's been telling you things," he said harshly. "Somebody pumped you full of information and then sent you out here to torment me. There aren't any real ghosts, I just have you to haunt me."

"I have no idea what you're talking about," she said. "I came here by accident..."

"I thought you were lured here by the ghost of my little sister." His voice was sharp and anguished in his relentless sarcasm.

She didn't react the way he expected her to. She

blinked, and her face softened. "You think Fiona is the ghost of your sister?"

He hated hearing the name on her lips, so matter-of-fact. He pushed away from the chair, afraid that for once in his life his phenomenal self-control would shatter. "My sister, Fiona," he snapped. "Sixteen when she died, with long white-blond hair and a ring on her finger. She drowned, with my parents, fifteen years ago, and I was the only one to survive. My father, who like all Irish fathers was called Da, and my mother Maeve, who happened to be the spitting image of my ancestor, Lady Fiona. Leaving me behind."

He expected shock and sorrow, even guilt. He expected her beautiful blue eyes to fill with tears. She was shocked, all right, and troubled. But not repentant. "How could your mother look like Lady Fiona?" she asked in that infuriatingly practical voice of hers. "The woman in the portrait is your father's ancestor, not your mother's."

"My mother's maiden name was O'Neal as well. They were third cousins."

"I thought the Catholic Church frowned on that sort of thing."

"The Catholic Church…" He realized suddenly that she'd distracted him. "For God's sake we're not talking about theological canon here. What the hell business is it of yours, anyway?"

She smiled up at him with endearing sweetness.

"Just trying to make conversation," she said serenely.

"You still haven't answered my question."

"What the hell business is it of mine?" she countered, her forehead wrinkled beneath her mop of red curls.

"No. Who told you about my family? Who gave you their names, who told you what they looked like, who sent you here to torment me?"

"No one," she said.

"I don't believe you."

"Trust is not one of your few virtues," she replied evenly. "Go about it the other way, then. Assuming I was fool enough to seek you out in a hurricane and almost drive off a cliff, assuming I arranged to have a tree fall on the car, knock me out and keep me a prisoner here, why don't you sit back and figure out who it was who could have sent me here? Who knows about your family, who would have filled me full of information?"

The rising frustration was almost worse than the pain he'd felt at her artless words. "No one," he said.

"'No one'?" she echoed.

"There's no one left alive who knew about my family. There's no one who could have told you those details."

He expected her full mouth to curve in triumph. Instead she looked disconcerted. "You mean I really saw them? Heard them?"

"It appears so."

"You mean there really are ghosts?" Her voice rose a bit, and outside the building winds howled in counterpoint.

"Haven't you been insisting on that ever since you got here?" he snapped in annoyance.

"I didn't...that is, I wasn't sure..." Her voice failed, and she looked absolutely stricken. And for some mad reason he wanted to comfort her, to tell her it was all right.

He was a fool and a half. He moved away from her, afraid that if he stayed too close he would touch her. Not in anger. He took a deep, calming breath, willing the anger, willing the desire to leave him. It wouldn't.

"We lived in Ireland," he said abruptly. "I was born over here, though, and we traveled a great deal. We'd planned to move to the States. My mother was second-generation American, and she missed her country. We were just waiting for the paperwork to go through when the four of us went out for a sail on a clear, bright day in October."

"I don't..."

"You don't want to hear the grim details?" he finished for her. "Too bad. You're the one who brought my family into this, you might at least learn why it's impossible for them to be here."

"Nothing's impossible," she said faintly.

He let out a bitter laugh. "You're younger than I thought," he said. "The storm came out of nowhere, and we were farther out than we realized. My father had lived all his life around the Irish Sea, but this storm was unnatural, fierce and demanding, and we knew we were all going to die. The waves came up and tossed the boat like it was a child's toy, and it sank without a trace, taking my sister and parents with it.''

"And what happened to you? Were you a better swimmer?''

He could tell her the truth and watch disbelief and horror cloud her open face. Or he could give her a part of it, the part he told most people. "Somehow or other I made it to shore," he said.

"But you were way out at sea," she protested. "In a storm. How could you swim that far?

"Miles," he said softly. "Miles and miles out to sea, with the wind screaming and the waves rising up like the wrath of God. And I have no idea how I got back to land. Someone said they saw a seal down by the water just before they saw me, and they thought one of them might have helped me, but I have my doubts." They were more than doubts—he knew the truth. As the years had passed, memory, more memory than he had ever wanted, had returned.

"The seal," she said in a dreamy voice. "Maybe it's the same one I saw in the water today. Maybe he's some kind of guardian angel—"

His harsh laugh interrupted her. "If there even was a seal, he lived off the Irish coast. There's no way he would have made his way across the Atlantic Ocean. Unless you're suggesting he took a plane.''

''I'm not suggesting anything.'' She managed to sound dignified.

''If a seal saved me, he's long dead on the other side of the sea. My family, as well. They died in Ireland, Katie Flynn, fifteen years ago. They wouldn't suddenly decide to cross the ocean and start haunting a perfect stranger when their own son would have given anything—'' He stopped as his voice grew harsher, and he cursed her and his own unexpected vulnerability.

''Ghosts can't cross the sea any more than seals can?'' Katie said gently. ''Who wrote that down in the Official Handbook for Ghosts? I've never been in Ireland, never seen you before yesterday, and yet I've seen your family. Maybe you simply haven't had the eyes to see them?''

That was a possibility he refused to consider. ''I don't believe in ghosts,'' he said in a voice as dead as his parents.

''What about a seal as your guardian angel? Would you consider that possibility?''

''No.''

She frowned. ''Then what do you believe in?''

He surveyed her for a long moment, willing to let her look into his eyes and see the depth of his pain and rage. He believed in the elegant curve of her high cheekbones, the soft tangle of red gold hair.

He believed in sin and the possibility of redemption for everyone but him. He believed in desire and the wrath of God, and he believed in his own doom.

He wasn't about to tell her that—she knew too much about him already. He didn't want her knowing how much he wanted her. "Absolutely nothing at all," he said in his deep voice.

She rose, and he knew a moment's terror that she would touch him, put her warm, soft, human hands on him, and he wouldn't be able to resist her. "That would be tragic indeed," she said, and she sounded annoyingly practical. "If I believed you for one moment. Which I don't."

He stayed where he was, looking up at her as she approached him. It gave him a lazy kind of advantage, and he was willing to take any that he could. "Why not?"

"Because you don't look like a man who's given up hope. If you were, you'd be dead."

Little did she know how close he'd come to it. How many times he'd started swimming, arcing through the icy Atlantic, heading out and hoping to simply sink out there beneath the black, heartless depths.

He hadn't yet. And for some damnable reason Katie Flynn was making him feel alive again. It was probably something as simple as lust, but it was enough. He wasn't ready to let go yet.

"What do you believe in?" she said again.

"Annoying little interlopers with red hair."

He was unprepared for her response. Her smile was utterly dazzling, lighting the huge, gloom-laden room. Outside the rain lashed against the windows as the storm closed down around them, inside there was a sudden glow. "That's something," she said. "Maybe they brought me here for a reason. To irritate you into dealing with life instead of hiding from it like a self-pitying hermit."

The words fell into the room like an ax cleaving through a fragile sapling. It took him a moment to speak, to be certain his voice would be steady and slightly mocking. "You must be a social worker in your real life," he said. "I suppose it's an ingrained habit, but I really don't need you analyzing me, telling me how to live my life. I do just fine on my own."

She looked stricken, but he suspected it wasn't his words that had wounded her. It was the unavoidable truth of her own.

"I'm sorry," she said. "That really was unforgivable of me. I do have a habit of interfering where I shouldn't."

He shrugged. "Some women are naturally controlling. They don't know how to leave well enough alone."

"I'm not a control freak," she protested hotly.

"Aren't you?"

"I just…have a habit of trying to make things better. I see a problem and I try to fix it."

"Not all problems can be fixed. Not all people can be fixed."

"I don't believe that."

He smiled grimly. "You're very young."

"Stop saying that! I'm twenty-eight. You can't be that much older than me."

"Not in years, perhaps," he said. "But in life experience I'm ancient."

"Living like a hermit for fifteen years doesn't provide a great deal of life experience."

"Do you always have to argue?" he demanded wearily.

"It runs in the blood. I'm Irish, you know."

"I know. So am I."

She grinned faintly. "Then we're well matched."

"No, we're not." The words had the finality of a death sentence, and for once she was silent, unable to come up with a bright response.

He wondered if she wanted him even half as much as he wanted her. He doubted it. The longer he was around her the thicker, deeper, more powerful his need for her. His hands shook with the need to touch her, and he knew that was the last thing he should, or could do. To touch her would be to doom her, as his family was doomed.

"No," she said finally. "I suppose not." She glanced around her, running a nervous hand through her rain-damp hair. "I should go up and change. I'm still wet from the rain. If you don't mind I'll just eat in my room tonight and keep out of your way. I've already been enough of an imposition."

"Mrs. Marvel doesn't need the inconvenience of serving two meals," he said, wondering why he wasn't taking the easy way out. Mrs. Marvel would do exactly what he told her to do, and he'd never been overly concerned with her well-being in the past. "You'll eat with me."

He half expected her to declaim something suitably dramatic like "I'd rather starve!" but she simply inclined her head. "Am I allowed to change out of these wet clothes? In the privacy of my room? Or would you rather I strip down right here?"

"I really don't care," he said, wondering if there was any way she could believe he was indifferent to her. She saw certain things much too clearly. In other areas she was blessedly, endearingly blind. She probably didn't have the faintest idea what kind of effect she was having on him. Apart from the irritation.

She smiled icily, heading for the door. "Then I'll be back in time for dinner," she said.

He didn't know what made him rise, move to the door ahead of her. His hand was already on the latch when she reached out for it, and she touched him, warmth against his icy cold, and it was like an electric shock coursing through his body.

She yanked her hand away, but it was too late, they were too close, and just for the moment he didn't want to fight it. He simply stood there, barring the door.

She took a deep, calming breath. "Look," she said. "I know you don't like me. You think I'm a mouthy, nosy American broad who won't leave you in peace, and you're right. It's not my nature to ignore it when people are in pain."

"I'm not in pain," he said tightly.

"Oh, yeah? Then you're the only one who doesn't realize it," she shot back. "But I'll leave you alone if you'd just let me. I'll disappear into my room and stay there until the storm passes, and then I'll be out of here, and you won't ever have to..." Her voice trailed off as he held the delicate gold chain in front of her eyes.

It was a stupid move on his part. He should have left it down in the bottom of the sea, trapped in the catch of the sodden purse that floated loosely in the submerged car. If he'd had any sense he wouldn't have gone after it in the first place, but he wanted to find out what made a cool, unsentimental creature like Katie Flynn cry.

It was a gold cross, very old, very Irish, bedecked with garnets. Its value was meager compared to some of the salvage he'd come up with over the years, but the gold chain had slipped around his sleek neck of its own accord, it seemed, and he'd brought it up from the depths of the sea with no real intention of handing it over to her.

And now it dangled between them, glinting in

the firelight, and she stared at it in hypnotic wonder. "How did you get it?" she whispered.

"I'm a diver."

"In this weather?" She reached up her hand to touch it, almost as if it were a holy relic, and he placed it in her palm, closing her fingers over it, feeling the warmth of her.

"I'm used to the waters around here," he said.

When she looked up there were tears in her wide blue eyes, and they were almost his undoing. "It was my grandmother's," she said. "It was the only thing I really treasured."

In another moment she would have flung herself in his arms, and he couldn't have stood that. "It was nothing," he said brusquely, stepping back, opening the door for her. Waiting for her to leave him in dubious peace.

She had no choice but to accept her dismissal, he'd seen to that. But she stopped and reached her hand up to touch his face.

He jerked back before she could make contact, and bright color stained her cheeks as she fell back in embarrassment. "Thank you," she said.

He watched her disappear down the darkened halls as night grew deep around them. She must have known he stood there, staring after her, but she didn't pause, didn't look back.

He let out a deep, strangled breath. He was only making things worse. Katie Flynn was a nosy, interfering, overimaginative, absolutely infuriating creature. He was also obsessed by her, so obsessed that he couldn't even begin to guess what she thought of him. Whether she was the slightest bit attracted to him, when he'd tried so hard to be unpleasant. Whether she felt the same kind of longing he did.

That longing would disappear, to be replaced by disbelief and horror if she knew the truth. There was no guardian angel watching over him in the form of a seal. No sleek brown animal had helped him to shore after the accident—he'd gotten there under his own steam.

No seal watched over him as he swam through the dangerous tides at Seal Point.

There was only O'Neal. Who until fifteen years ago had had no idea that he was part of an ancient race, an ancient curse. The roan; half man, half seal, wholly cursed.

Cursed to watch his family die in front of him and be unable to save them. Cursed to live a half life, alone and embittered.

Cursed.

Chapter Nine

Someone had been in her room. Katie knew it with
a passionate certainty, just as she knew it was no
friendly specter. Whoever had come in while she
was gone had left no trace, no sign of their trespass,
and yet she knew. Someone had touched the bed
where she lay, someone had run their all-too-human
hands along her discarded clothing. Someone had
been watching her.

It was absurd, she reminded herself. She'd imagined eyes following her from the moment she even
neared this place. She'd seen the seal watching her,
the faded eyes of ghosts that she didn't even believe
in. Why should the sense that she was being spied
on feel like anything new and disturbing?

Night had fallen, a thick dark blanket smothering
the deep-set windows, and the sound of the rain was
like a muffled thunder. Katie didn't even bother to
try to look out. There would be nothing to see, just
darkness, and maybe a ghostly face staring back at
her.

She sat cross-legged on the bed, shivering in the cool dampness of the room. O'Neal was right, uncannily so. The ghosts and apparitions didn't frighten her in the least. It was something else, something cold and dark and evil that lived in the heart of this house, that unnerved her.

Did it live in O'Neal? It couldn't be Mrs. Marvel—her cozy warmth and welcome ruled out any unfriendly intent. Willie was another matter, an excruciatingly uncomfortable one. Katie had always accepted those around her without passing judgment, and Willie's limited abilities should have only made him pitiable.

But he frightened her. And why should she assume he was as devoid of evil as he was devoid of intellect?

She glanced through the murky light to the huge dresser. A pile of faded clothing lay folded neatly, and Katie breathed a sigh of relief. It had been Mrs. Marvel, bringing her fresh clothes. Not some evil intruder after all.

She changed, hurriedly, knowing she was being absurdly superstitious. No one could see her as she pulled off the damp clothes Mrs. Marvel had lent her, replacing them with an equally faded, loose dress that came down to her ankles. No one would want to see her. And yet she found herself looking over her shoulder, nervous, edgy. Looking for a human intruder, not a ghostly one.

There were fresh toiletries in the bathroom—a

comb, toothbrush and toothpaste, and she did her best to make herself demure and presentable. It was little wonder O'Neal thought she was some sort of harpy, with her flyaway hair and her pale face. She pinched her cheeks to bring some color into them, then stared back. Demure was probably too much of a stretch, but at least she looked relatively lady-like if she was going to be forced to have dinner with O'Neal.

She couldn't imagine why he really wanted her company. He'd made it more than clear that she was an imposition, one he wanted gone. Maybe he was afraid she'd start exploring again. Maybe he didn't want her to see any more ghosts.

She would have preferred to do without them herself, she thought, pulling on a pair of kneesocks that had seen better days but were at least blessedly warm. But the ghosts seemed to have an affinity for her. Just her luck that they'd choose now to appear.

The table was set for two in the library, with sandwiches and hot coffee already poured, and the fire was burning brightly. Outside, the storm raged, a steady thudding roar that had become almost sub-liminal. Inside, O'Neal sat in the huge leather chair, his long legs stretched out in front of him, sound asleep.

She closed the door silently behind her. The Marvels were in the kitchen—Katie could hear Mrs. Marvel's raised voice as she spoke to her son. She was alone with O'Neal, and she felt like one of the ghosts. Watching, unseen, a creature neither present nor absent. She moved silently into the room and sat in the chair opposite him, watching him.

It annoyed her that he was so breathtakingly beautiful. He was slightly older than she'd thought, the lines around his eyes told of years of squinting into bright sunlight, and the grim brackets around his mouth held no memory of smiles. His mouth was well shaped, the lips narrow yet oddly sensuous. His nose might have been too pronounced, and yet it merely strengthened his elegant face. His dark hair, a rich seal brown, framed his face, and his skin was tanned, smooth, the glorious skin of the British Isles.

It was just as well his eyes were closed. It was his eyes that she found most unnerving.

She didn't want to look at his body, but she told herself she was a fool to avoid it. A body was nothing more than a shell—he was a man like other men. Two legs, though his were long and strong-looking beneath the faded black jeans. Two arms, long as well, with the usual two hands attached. Beautiful hands, she had to admit. Hands that would know how to touch, to stroke, to gentle a wild creature and tame her.

He was lean and muscled, with a flat stomach, slightly bony shoulders, and narrow hips. He had the kind of body she used to lust after in the movies. She was too sensible to lust after him now.

After all, it was the man inside who counted, not the sum of undeniably attractive parts.

He'd kissed her, she remembered suddenly. Kissed her eyelids, not her mouth, and she wondered why she'd blotted that particular fact out of her mind. And why he'd come so close. Had he been drunk? Trying to scare her? If so, it hadn't worked.

She wanted to taste his mouth. She wanted him to open his green eyes and look at her. She wanted him to touch her face, her mouth. She wanted...

His eyes were open, she realized with a chill that washed across her heated skin, and she wondered if he could see the fevered thoughts that had been running through her brain. Thoughts she'd never felt before, for any man.

"How long have you been sitting there?" His voice startled her, smoky, with the faint Irish lilt. She'd forgotten that his voice was one of the most seductive things about him, as powerful as his elegant hands and his haunted eyes. And his thin, sensuous mouth.

"Not long," she said.

"And what were you thinking?" He didn't move, but lounged in the old leather chair, at ease, watching her as intently as she'd watched him.

"That I'm absolutely starving."

He laughed at her pragmatic answer, the sound startling in the stillness of the old room. He wasn't a man who laughed often.

"Help yourself to the sandwiches. Mrs. Marvel is an excellent cook, and I'm sure she's grateful to have an appreciative audience for once. I'm not terribly interested in food."

"What are you interested in?" she blurted out.

He had glanced away, into the fire, but her words drew him back, and his eyes met hers for a long, breathless moment, and she heard the word "you" as clear as a bell inside her head.

But he hadn't spoken. He simply shrugged. "My solitude."

She touched the cross that hung around her neck. "And diving."

His smile was faintly twisted but not without humor. "That's more of a necessity than an interest."

"Why?"

"People lose things," he said carelessly. "I pick them up. It must be part of my tidy nature."

"Do you always return everything?"

He shook his head. "Many of things I find belonged to people who've been dead for decades, even centuries. There's a roomful of stuff in the basement. Most of it completely worthless, of course."

"Most of it?"

"The rest keeps me quite comfortably."

"You mean you find treasure? Pirates' gold?" She knew she sounded incredibly naive, but she couldn't help it. Visions of Errol Flynn movies popped into her head.

"There weren't many pirates around the coast of Maine."

"Is this the only place you dive? Do you never leave here?"

"Actually I'm fond of the Caribbean. The warm water is very soothing. I've found some interesting stuff around Barbados." He tilted his head sideways and assessed her. "Some nice, gaudy jewelry that would appeal to you."

"You think I have gaudy taste?" She should have been incensed, but the faint, teasing note in his voice was inescapably seductive.

"I think you could be persuaded to have magnificently gaudy taste." His voice was soft, luring her.

She bit her lip. "I'll have you know I've been sedate and tasteful all my life."

"Poor Katie Flynn," he murmured. "Haven't you ever wanted to run away with the gypsies? Join the circus? Dance on a tabletop?"

"Not particularly," she said. Shutting out her childhood fantasies ruthlessly.

"Haven't you ever wanted to drape yourself in jewels and nothing more? Creamy pearls and sinuous jade?" His voice was what was sinuous, and she had to fight to keep from falling under its spell.

"Sounds drafty," she said.

"I don't know. It sounds quite…hot…to me."

She could feel the heat rising beneath the faded dress, warming her stomach, her breasts, making her skin tingle beneath his languid gaze. "What are you doing?" she asked sharply.

"What do you mean?"

"For the last day and a half you've been scowling at me and trying to get rid of me. Suddenly you're talking about romping naked in jewels. Is this rampant sexuality another attempt to scare me away?"

"Does it scare you, Katie?" His voice was low and beguiling. "Why should you be afraid of sex?"

"I'm not!" Her voice was unnaturally loud in the quiet room. "I'm not," she repeated in a calmer voice. "And why are we talking about sex?"

"We weren't," he said. "You brought up the subject. I was just talking about jewels. Plunder."

There was something incredibly erotic about that word. Plunder. She'd never really considered it before, but coming from his mouth it did strange, unnerving things to her.

"I'm not afraid of sex, nudity, pirates, plundered jewels, ghosts or you," she said firmly. Lying through her teeth.

And he knew it. He leaned back, a faintly mocking smile on his beautiful, distant face. "If you say so, Katie Flynn. Does that mean you don't want to see my treasure room and my hoard of salvage?"

"It doesn't mean any such thing. As you pointed out earlier, we're trapped here for the time being, and life can get boring. As long as you feed me

I'm ready for just about anything. Just don't expect me to model your pearls for you.''

He only smiled.

HE WASN'T QUITE SURE what had made him tease her like that. Flirt with her. Part of it was waking up to find her watching him. She wanted him. It was no ego fantasy on his part, or merely wishful thinking. She was obsessed with him. And she was frightened of him, far more than she was of the ghostly apparitions that appeared to no one but her.

He still wasn't sure that he believed in her particular ghosts. There could be reasonable explanations for all the fantasies she'd concocted. She might just be an incredibly suggestible creature, easily able to conjure a vision out of an idea.

He wondered how suggestible she would be when it came to sex.

He'd opened his eyes to find her watching him, and he'd immediately gotten hard. It surprised him—he wasn't used to his body responding with such immediate, blatant need. Katie Flynn seemed to have that unfortunate effect on him. And she wasn't as immune to it all as she liked to think.

She also wasn't ready to come romping into his bed, he knew that with depressing certainty. She wasn't a woman who tumbled in and out of beds, in and out of affairs with the breeziness of her eminently practical nature. Beneath her sturdy nononsense demeanor was the soul of a dreamer, and she was a woman who needed to be wooed, needed to be loved, needed to be slowly and cleverly seduced until she was unable to resist.

He didn't have that much time, thank God. She'd be gone by tomorrow—this damned storm couldn't last forever. He'd been through countless nor'easters, even a hurricane or two in the time he'd spent on the Maine coast, and this particular storm had to be the most violent he'd yet encountered. It couldn't get any worse, it could only weaken.

Or so he hoped.

His time with Katie was limited, and he was safe. She wasn't going to discover his unbearable secret. If Mrs. Marvel and Willie had no idea, after living with him for more than twelve years, then no chance-met stranger was going to figure out the unimaginable.

He could flirt with her. He could tease her, annoy her, even touch her if he dared risk it. Tomorrow she'd be gone, and he could retreat back into his hermetic existence.

He would take her down to the vaults and show her what he'd never shown another living soul. Mrs. Marvel knew of the locked rooms, of course, and there was no guarantee she'd never found her way inside. But she wasn't interested in long-lost treasure and pirate booty. She was a practical woman, only interested in practical things.

But Katie Flynn was a dreamer. Drape her in pearls, and she would glow. Cover her in emeralds and rubies, and she could be a pirate's captive and he—

Had definitely too much time on his hands to waste on erotic fantasies. He had one more night with her before the storm finally faded—there was no way it could last any longer. He could push things as far as she'd let him, knowing that in the end she would never make the mistake of going to bed with him. He'd be safe to play with her, tease her, tease himself. And tomorrow she'd be gone, and he'd be alone again. His secrets safe.

"Do you have anything else to wear?" he asked, giving her clothes a derisive glance. In truth, the long, billowing dress draped around her quite nicely, flowing with the curves on her body, but since he'd last seen it clasped snugly around Mrs. Marvel's sturdy frame he had a difficult time fantasizing about it.

"Not unless you brought up my suitcases as well as my grandmother's cross," she said. "Mrs. Marvel was kind enough to lend me some of her stuff, but I can't very well be choosy."

He remembered the suitcases. They'd tumbled open with the force of the car hitting the ocean floor, and the rough waves had tossed the contents along miles of oceanfront. Besides, he liked her in dresses. "It's cold down there," he said. "Eat something while I find you one of my sweaters, and then I'll take you down."

She opened her mouth to protest, then shut it

again, and he wondered what it was that troubled her. The thought of descending into the bowels of the old mansion, or wearing one of his old sweaters? She could hardly protest eating, when it seemed to be one of her obsessions.

She didn't protest when he handed her the thick Aran sweater he'd worn yesterday. She pulled it over her head, shivering slightly as she shook her red hair loose. The sleeves came beyond her fingertips and she rolled them up. She looked utterly beguiling in the enveloping folds of the sweater, and he regretted giving it to her. It was too late now.

She stroked the dark chocolate wool that glimmered in the firelight. "What a wonderful color," she said. "It looks like mink. What did they use to dye the wool?"

"It's not dyed. It comes from the wool of a black sheep. I found the idea entertaining."

She looked up at him. "Do you see yourself as a black sheep?"

"I'm not wild enough to be a black sheep. More a lost soul, I think." He glanced at her feet. "Do you have any shoes?"

He already knew the answer, and he pulled a pair of Wellies from the corner by the door. She'd swim in them, but at least they'd provide her feet some protection.

She slipped them on, then looked at him brightly. "I'm ready for treasure hunting," she said.

She wasn't, but he'd learned early on that Katie Flynn wasn't a woman to give in to fear or uneasiness. He picked up an oil lamp to light their way, then reached out and took her hand. "Come along," he said.

Her hand was warm in his cool one, and he half expected her to pull away. He could feel the need to escape warring within her. And then her fingers curled around his, with alarming trust, and the first tendril of regret sank into his bones.

"Lead on," she said.

"I DON'T THINK we can wait, Willie." Mrs. Marvel stood in the doorway of her son's tidy little room, eyeing him with her usual grim expression. "I don't know if we can afford to wait until the storm is over. Listen to the man. I've never heard him sound so—"

"Happy?" Willie suggested.

Mrs. Marvel shot him a disapproving glare. "What has happiness to do with anything? O'Neal sounds like he's come alive again, and it's that girl's fault. Even if we get rid of her the damage may have already been done. Our time here may soon be over."

"That's all right. You told me we've got enough money put away—"

"There's no such thing as 'enough money,'" she corrected him. "This was a comfortable spot for the likes of us. O'Neal doesn't even pay attention to all the things he has down there, and he just keeps gathering more. We could have been obscenely rich if we could have held out for a few more years.''

''Why can't we?''

Mrs. Marvel sighed, a long-suffering sigh. ''Because O'Neal is going to start noticing. Once we get rid of the girl he may go back to the way he was, but I wouldn't count on it. He might even decide to go after her.''

''But she'll be dead, Ma.''

''I know that, Willie. But he won't. And if he leaves here, he might hear rumors about the two of us. And he won't be around to keep bringing up riches from the ocean.''

''He's gone before and come back.''

''This time, Willie, he won't come back. We can't afford to let that happen.''

Willie scratched his head. ''What are we going to do, Ma?

Mrs. Marvel sighed. ''It may not be too late. I want you to kill her, Willie. I want you to do it quickly and neatly, no noise or fuss, and then I want you to dispose of her body where no one will ever find it. We'll tell O'Neal she was able to get a ride to town, and chances are he'll forget about her. If we're lucky.''

''But, Ma, you promised me,'' Willie protested.

''Not this time, Willie. This one will have to be a job, not a pleasure. The money comes first. I can count on you, my boy? You won't let me down?''

Willie nodded reluctantly. "Ain't fair," he muttered.

"Life isn't fair. I want you to kill her, Willie. Kill her tonight."

"Yes, ma'am," Willie said in his docile voice. "Tonight."

Chapter Ten

If Katie had thought the huge old mansion was cold and dark, it was nothing compared to the winding stone staircase that seemed to lead down to the very heart of the earth. She could smell the salt of the sea, the fresh scent of water as she followed him down, led by his hand and the flickering light of the lantern. Visions of old horror movies danced in her head. She couldn't remember exactly what she'd heard about Bluebeard. Hadn't he had a dozen wives that he murdered and kept locked in a cellar?

Or maybe it was an attic. Besides, O'Neal was hardly likely to murder her, no matter how annoying he found her. Neither was he likely to add her to a long list of deceased brides.

"Where are we going?" she asked, and her voice echoed oddly in the narrow stone tunnel. "It feels as if we're under the sea."

He didn't pause or look back at her, but the feel of his hand grasping hers was still strong. He was growing warmer now—he'd always seemed so cold to her, as cold as the sea. But even as they descended farther into the darkness he seemed to warm to her touch, a fact she found disquieting. Disturbing. Arousing.

"You're closer to the truth than you realize. There are caves criss-crossing beneath the promontory, and some of the pathways run parallel to the stairs. When the tide is particularly high the floors get wet."

She glanced down at her feet in their clumsy rubber boots, but it was too dark to tell whether the dampness had risen or not. "Aren't you worried about the place collapsing? I mean, given the storm and all?"

"It's built on granite, and it's stood for more than a hundred years. I don't think one bad storm is going to send it toppling into the sea."

"It's more than a bad storm. The last weather report I heard talked about a hurricane. Hurricane Margo."

"If I believed every panic-stricken weather bulletin, I wouldn't be living out here at the edge of nowhere," O'Neal said calmly.

"It was supposed to be a big one. Category four at least, with storm surges and catastrophic winds..."

"And how long ago did you hear that? Days ago, it had to have been. It's probably gone out to sea, and the storms we're getting are just the outer edges of it, the remnants hitting land.''

"Maybe," Katie said.

He paused, looking back at her. "You don't seem particularly distressed by the notion."

"I love storms. Though if this were a full-blown hurricane I think I'd rather watch it from some safe motel that gets the Weather Channel."

"Some safe motel would probably lose their power, and you'd have no idea what's going on. If by any remote chance there's still some strength left in your hurricane, you couldn't pick a safer place to be. We're entirely self-sufficient. We don't need electricity, we have no radios or televisions so there's nothing to miss. There's plenty of food, plenty of candles and lanterns, and the house is made of stone, built on solid rock. There's no way even the most powerful hurricane could endanger it."

"Knock on wood," she muttered, glancing around her. There was no wood to be seen.

"You don't believe me?"

"I just get superstitious when someone says something can't possibly happen. It seems like Fate takes that as a personal challenge."

For a moment he said nothing, then he shook his head. "I'd forgotten how Irish you are."

"Don't tell me I remind you of your mother," she begged.

"Not Maeve. She was far too levelheaded. And

you're not romantic like Fiona. No, I think you're more like my Great Aunt Moira. She used to hold séances and converse with the ghost of Charles Parnell. She also used to slap my hand with a ruler if she thought I was being naughty. She was just like you.''

"If I were going to talk with dead Irishmen I'd probably prefer Yeats or Synge and not some adulterous politician. And I have absolutely no desire to slap you.''

His smile was brief and disbelieving. "Don't you, now? Why should I find that hard to believe?''

"Maybe because you know that most people who meet you end up wanting to clobber you,'' she suggested helpfully.

"Not most people. Most women.''

"And you meet so many in your current lifestyle?''

He laughed, and the sound was soft and surprisingly pleasant in the stone passageway. "True enough.'' He turned and moved onward, and she followed him, wishing she still had his hand to hold on to.

He stopped in front of a heavy steel door and handed her the lantern. There were at least three different locks, all of recent vintage, and she watched in fascination, peering through the darkness.

The door opened with a satisfyingly sepulchral creak, and he took the lantern back from her, holding it high to light their way. The bright flame had died back a bit, providing a weaker flicker of light, but it was enough to illuminate O'Neal's treasure trove.

"Oh," Katie said, halting in the midst of the room and staring around in astonishment.

"Disappointed?" O'Neal murmured. "Were you expecting Blackbeard's pirate hoard?"

She shook her head, momentarily silenced. She had expected something out of a pirate movie—chests of jewels and gold spilling all over the place, cutlasses and skeletons in artful array.

This was like a curator's room from a museum. There were gold pieces, certainly, and piles of jewelry. There were also bright brass spyglasses, shards of pottery, ancient instruments barely damaged by their sojourn in the depths of the sea. Without thinking, she bypassed the pile of jewels that glowed dimly in the light and went to touch an ancient stoneware jug, adorned with pale blue hummingbirds.

"This is beautiful," she said, stroking it with loving hands. Beside it lay an ancient telescope, still shiny despite its immersion, and she picked it up with reverent care. "These things are amazing."

He was watching her with an odd expression on his face, but she'd accepted the fact that there was no way to tell what he was thinking. "You're interested in antiques?"

"I'm fascinated by things people actually used,"

she said, setting the brass tube down again. "I like to think about their lives, their cares, who they loved, who they hated."

"People wore jewelry, too."

She glanced over at the glittering pile of gold and gems. "I suppose so," she said. "My ancestors were decent, hardworking common folk. I think they were more likely to care about a good plough than a string of pearls."

He set the lantern down on the table and picked up one of the strands. They were like nothing she'd ever seen before—a shimmering, luminous gray-black that seemed to glow with a life on its own.

"And you're more interested in an old telescope than a strand of the finest, rarest of black pearls?" His voice was soft, seductive, as he held them out to her.

She wished she could deny their appeal, but she was, above all things, honest. "They're beautiful," she said, making no effort to touch them. "I'm surprised they survived in the ocean."

"Don't be silly, pearls come from the ocean in the first place. It only makes them glow more brightly. These aren't as lustrous as they should be, of course."

"Why not? They look utterly magnificent as they are."

"Pearls are unlike any other jewelry. They need to be worn. They pick up a sheen and luster from a woman's skin. When they lie in darkness, untouched, their glow fades.''

"They don't need a woman's skin,'' she shot back. "You're not going to tell me that estrogen makes them shiny—I won't believe it. Why don't you wear them?'' She was being deliberately cranky. She wanted those black pearls. They were huge, sumptuous, frankly erotic, and she wanted them lying next to her skin, taking her warmth, glowing with her life. And she would have died rather than admit it.

O'Neal merely smiled faintly. "They're not my style. Turn around.''

"Why?''

"So I can put them on you. I told you, they need to be worn.''

"Not by me.'' It was getting darker and darker in the windowless stone room, and she couldn't figure out why. He'd set the lantern down by the door, and no one had come near it.

"By you,'' he said, and put his arms around her neck.

She couldn't escape—he'd already lifted up her mass of hair and begun fastening the string of black pearls. His hands were cool against the warmth of her skin, but the pearls seemed to be alive, vibrating, hot, against the soft, vulnerable skin of her neck.

She held her breath, she wasn't sure why, sneaking a look up at him out of lowered eyes. He was so close she could see where he'd nicked himself shaving that morning, she could see the faint gold flecks in his sea green eyes. She could feel the warmth of him, the heat of his body, the softness of his breath, and if he didn't hurry up she'd probably pass out from lack of oxygen....

He stepped back, and she let out her breath with a strangled gasp. "Very nice," he murmured, surveying her with lazy interest. "They suit you."

She couldn't stop herself from touching them. They rested against her vulnerable throat like rich black grapes, and for a moment her fingers curled around them, tempted to rip them off. It was more than a necklace. It was a claiming, whether he knew it or not. And she was afraid to be claimed.

"I can't..." she said, but her voice came out with no more than a whisper.

"They'll die here in the darkness," he said. "Untouched, unwanted, their light will go out and they'll be lost forever. Take them."

He wasn't talking about the exotic black pearls. She wasn't thinking about the pearls when she reached out her hand to him. He flinched, as if afraid of her touch, but he didn't step back, and her fingertips brushed the long dark hair away from his cheek.

The darkness closed down about them like a trap as the lantern flickered and went out. A moment later the door slammed, and they were sealed inside the stone room, like lovers in an ancient tomb.

Katie stumbled back, away from him, in sudden panic. "What happened?"

"The lantern went out. I can't imagine why—Mrs. Marvel always keeps them filled and trimmed." He sounded slightly bored.

Boredom was the furthest thing from Katie's mind. She felt as if she were suffocating, shut in the dark and damp with a stranger, and she forced herself to take a deep, calming breath. "I bet you're the kind of date who always ran out of gas on the way home." She managed to make her voice caustic.

"This isn't a date," he said, "and I don't play games."

It was just as well the place was pitch-black—even someone with his unexpectedly strong night vision wouldn't be able to see the hot blush that rose to her cheeks.

"I thought I heard the door slam," she said.

He was moving away from her with unerring grace, deftly avoiding the tables in the darkness. She could hear the useless tug at the doorknob, followed by his muffled curse.

"We're locked in." His voice was flat, unemotional.

"How could we be? You had the keys..."

"I left them in the door when we came in."

"That wasn't particularly clever of you."

"I've been a bit...distracted these past few

days.'' His voice moved across the darkness, touching her.

"But surely you knew there was a chance the door could slam shut? Gravity or the wind or..."

"There's no wind down here," he said. "And the door is hung perfectly—it stays where it's supposed to, unless it has a little help."

"What do you mean by that?"

"I mean someone locked us in here. Someone tampered with the lamp. Maybe one of your ghosts?" He didn't bother to keep the faint contempt from his voice.

"They can't," she said.

"Really? You're an expert on ghosts, I presume?" he countered.

"Not really. I just don't think they're capable of actually touching things. I think they're more of a shadow, or a dream. Not something physical."

"That's unfortunate. If the ghosts of my family were haunting this place I'd think they'd be likely to help me out of here if they were capable of doing so."

"Not if they knew you really well," Katie muttered, unable to resist.

He made no sound, and there was absolutely no reason why she thought he was smiling at her snotty crack. She just had the strong sense that he was.

"The Marvels will realize we've disappeared and come after us," he said, and his voice was closer than it had been before. She hadn't heard him approach in the inky darkness, and she jumped, startled.

"Did they see us come down here?"

"Mrs. Marvel doesn't miss much."

"But if you didn't lock us in here, and the ghosts didn't, doesn't that somehow suggest that the Marvels are the ones who locked the door?"

"Why would they?"

"Don't ask me!" she said, and her carefully squashed down nervousness was bubbling up into her voice. "But there's no one else here, is there? No crazy wife locked in the attic?"

He was standing only inches away—she could feel him there—but he made no effort to touch her. "No crazy wife in the attic. Who did you think you were, Jane Eyre?"

"You do a pretty good imitation of Mr. Rochester," she retorted. *Don't touch me,* she thought desperately. *Please don't touch me.*

"You're a romantic," he said, and in the darkness his voice was cool and unemotional. "I'm not a gothic hero, and you're not a beleaguered governess."

"Of course I'm not," she said sharply.

"And you aren't in love with me."

"Of course I'm not," she said again, hoping she sounded thoroughly horrified. "I don't even know you, and what I know I don't like."

"Exactly," he said.

"As long as we understand each other," she said, sounding exactly like a Victorian governess.

"We do," he said.

"Then I think I'll just have a seat on the floor and wait for the Marvels to rescue us...." She'd barely begun to sink to the hard stone when his hands found her, caught her in the darkness and hauled her up.

"The floor is wet," he said flatly. "The sea is coming in."

She froze. Entirely aware of his hands still on her arms, entirely aware of his body so close to hers. "How could that be?"

She felt rather than saw him shrug. "I'm not denying there's a bad storm out there," he said in a distant voice. "Bad enough that there's a storm surge, and water is coming up higher than usual."

"How high? Is it going to fill this room with us inside, unable to escape?"

"You've seen too many movies. There's barely an inch of water on the floor, and it would take hours and hours for it to come all the way up. By then the Marvels will have realized where we are."

"Unless they put us here in the first place."

"Why would they do that? Willie may be a little off, but there's no harm in him. And Mrs. Marvel is an absolute paragon of stern New England rectitude. She's totally incapable of evil."

"No one's incapable of evil," Katie said in a small voice.

He said nothing. A moment later he dropped his hands, and she heard the faint, telltale slosh of water as he stepped back from her. "Maybe you'd better climb up on one of the counters," he said.

"I thought the water wasn't going to rise that high before we were rescued."

"It isn't. But you said you wanted to sit down, so the safest, driest place for that is the counter." Before she knew what he was doing his hands had gone around her waist and he'd hoisted her up with a muffled grunt, setting her down on the solid wood counter with a decided thump.

He didn't move away. It brought her up to his level, and she realized that at some point she'd steadied herself by putting her hands on his shoulders. And she hadn't let go.

She jerked away, and something went crashing to the floor behind her. "I'm sorry," she gasped.

"Don't be." His hands left her, and his voice was strained. "I'll go wait over by the door and see if I can hear anyone coming."

Without thinking she reached out for him, catching the soft, loose cotton of his shirt in her hands. "Don't," she said.

"There's nothing to be afraid of." He sounded almost unnaturally calm. His hands covered hers, pulling them away and setting them back on the counter. And then he moved away, swiftly, as if he was trying to escape from her.

She pulled her legs up, wrapping her arms around

them, thoroughly rebuffed—and glad of it, she told herself. For heaven's sake, the man was acting as if she'd made a pass at him, when all she'd wanted...all she'd needed...

She didn't know what she wanted or needed. The sunlight, maybe, when she hadn't seen the sun in days. Her freedom, away from this dark, haunted place.

But away from this place would be away from O'Neal. And annoying, high-handed, infuriating as he might be, she didn't want to walk away from him.

"Tell me about my sister." His voice was so quiet, carrying across the room, that for a moment she wasn't sure she'd heard him speak.

But he had, and she knew without asking what he wanted to know. "She looked pretty," she said in a very gentle voice. "She looked happy. Almost peaceful, and yet..."

"And yet?" he echoed, his voice strained.

"Slightly naughty. Like someone with a secret that she was just dying to share. Like she wanted to tell me something." She peered toward him in the darkness, but she couldn't even see his shadow. "I thought you didn't believe me."

"I don't. I'd still prefer to hear your fantasies are pleasant ones."

"For my sake, or Fiona's?"

There was a sharp intake of breath, almost pained sounding. "For both of you," he said.

She closed her eyes, and for a moment she could almost see Fiona in the darkness, standing there watching them, an expression of supreme annoyance on her pale, youthful face. *Don't just sit there,* came a voice inside her head. *Do something.*

Katie opened her eyes, banishing the image from her consciousness. This tiny, locked room was crowded enough with the two of them—she didn't need any bothersome ghosts in there as well. She'd get along without an adolescent girl's helpful determination.

A crash sounded from the far wall, followed by the sound of breaking glass.

"What the hell was that?" O'Neal demanded roughly.

"I don't—" Something went sailing past her head, barely missing her, and she let out a shriek, leaping off the counter. Directly into two inches of rising seawater.

"It's getting deeper," she said in a panicked voice.

"Yes."

"We're going to die," she said.

"No." He was there, touching her, and she started to pull away, when something hit her directly between the shoulder blades, hit her hard, and sent her falling against him, so that he had no choice but to catch her, no choice but to put his arms around her. No choice but to put his mouth against hers.

And she was lost.

Chapter Eleven

He shouldn't be kissing her, and he knew it. Just as he knew there was no way he was going to stop once he'd started. She tasted of coffee and wine, she tasted of cinnamon and honey. And she was warm in the dank cold of the tomblike room. Warm and vibrant and alive. He could feel her heart pounding furiously against the soft material of her dress, and he reached a hand up between them and pressed it between her breasts, against her heartbeat, trying to draw the feel of it, the sound of it, through his skin into his very heart.

She didn't want to be kissing him, either, and yet she put her arms around his neck and clung to him. Maybe she was frightened of the rising water or the noises in the room. Maybe she was frightened of him. It didn't matter. All that mattered was her warm, soft body pressed up against his as the water crept higher and higher.

He should back away, and he knew it, but his hands wouldn't release her, his mouth wouldn't let go. He wanted to breathe her very breath as well, he wanted to pull her into him and absorb her like a warm blanket of love and compassion.

He moved his mouth away from hers, just for a moment, and her voice was small and pained. "Please don't," she said. But her hands clung to his shoulders tightly, and she rose on tiptoes and pressed her mouth against his, ignoring her own plea for mercy.

He could have stopped. She wanted him to stop, he wanted to stop, and it would have taken so little to step back, set her away from him, retreat to a corner and await rescue or drowning, he didn't give a damn which.

It would be the wise thing to do. To relinquish what he could never have. But the room was too dark, the night too cold, and she was more temptation than he had ever held in his entire life. And he couldn't let her go.

He caught her face in his hands and tilted it up to meet his. Her mouth opened willingly enough, but she seemed startled when he used his tongue, thrusting inside the warm sweet depth of her mouth, seeking some kind of haven. She liked it, though. He could tell by the faint, sweet sound she made, by the shiver that ran through her body, by the way her hands clung to him.

He wanted her. No matter how crazy and dangerous it was, he wanted her. Wanted to lie with her, sleep with her, make love with her. To taste every part of her body, to make her weep with pleasure.

He could feel the water, lapping around his ankles now, icy cold from the depths of the sea. He should probably be concentrating on a way to escape the storeroom, rather than kissing this totally inconvenient and annoying woman, but right then there was nothing he would rather do. The door was solid steel, the locks were burglar-proof, even if he'd ever acquired the dubious skill of picking locks, and the room was so far beneath the main floor of the house, with solid layers of rock between, that shouting for help would be a waste of time and breath.

He could survive under water for a relatively long time, but Katie would die. Of shock, hypothermia or drowning. One of those would carry her off. Carry her off as his family had been carried off, drowning in the black depths of the ocean.

He forced himself to pull away, back away from her in the darkness, the water sloshing noisily. With his night-trained eyes he could just see her, though he knew he would have disappeared into the blackness. She put a hand up to her mouth, and she was shaking.

"We shouldn't be doing this," he said. "I have to get us out of here."

She didn't argue with him. She turned away from him, wrapping her arms around her body to ward off the growing chill. "How?"

The calm sense of her question was as bracing as the icy water. As far as he could figure, there was no way out, but he wasn't about to tell her that. He couldn't afford to have a hysterical woman on his hands.

"I'll find a way."

"There is no way out." She was very calm. So much for his notion of hysterical women. "Is there?"

He considered lying to her, then dismissed the notion. "No," he said. "Not unless the Marvels come for us."

He heard her deep, shaky breath from across the pitch-black room. And then she turned and faced him. "Then I don't see any reason why we shouldn't do it," she said. And she waded through the water, leaned her body against his and put her arms around his neck.

He was a fool, but he couldn't help himself. He slid his hands up her long, sleek thighs, bringing the loose, flowered dress with them. She kissed him, and he realized she was singularly unused to kissing. He didn't care. He simply wrapped himself around her, drowning in the untutored grace of her mouth, her arms.

She was so alive. So strong, so warm beneath the loose dress, and he wanted to touch her, everywhere, to feel the heat of her flesh warming his. He'd been cold for so very, very long, and he needed the fire of her. Right or wrong, he was going to take her. There was no way he could fight it any longer.

The pounding on the door echoed through the damp tomb like the wrath of God, and he froze. "O'Neal!" Mrs. Marvel bellowed urgently. "Are you in there?"

He didn't want to set her away from him, but he had no choice. "We're here, Mrs. Marvel," he called out, carefully moving Katie away from him. "Have you got the keys?"

"They're still in the locks. Give me a moment, sir, and I'll have you out of there in a jiffy."

"I guess we're not going to drown after all." Katie's voice was shaky in the darkness.

He felt shaky, as well. Close to drowning, and he was a man unlike other men, a man who could not drown. But he'd felt carried away on a deep, rich wave of longing, and he could have given up, gone under, quite peacefully.

"Not tonight, anyway." He sounded calm, almost cynical, as if the taste of her mouth didn't linger and taunt him.

The door pushed open against the rising water, and a shallow light filled the room. Mrs. Marvel's sturdy bulk stood in the shadows beyond the lantern, and he wondered why he wasn't more grateful at being rescued.

"The water's rising fast, sir," she said. "There's no telling how high it will climb. Do you want me to see about moving some of this stuff to higher ground? I can have Willie down here in no time.''

"There's no need, Mrs. Marvel," he said, taking the lantern from her and holding it up so that Katie could make her way through the water. "All these things have already spent a great deal of time under water—a little more won't hurt them.'' He glanced at Katie's pale, strained face as she moved past, her clothes brushing against him. "Are you all right?''

"Fine," she said lightly. "I think I just need a good night's sleep. You're certain we're not in any danger here? If the water is filling the basement won't it damage the foundations?''

"The foundation is solid rock. We're safe, Katie. Go to bed, and when you wake up in the morning the storm will probably have passed, the sun will be shining, and you can be on your way.''

She stopped and looked up at him out of still, blue eyes, and there was knowledge and sadness in them. It was nothing compared to how she would look at him if she ever knew the truth, he thought, steeling himself. She was better off away from here, away from him, away from things she couldn't believe and would never want to experience.

"That would be nice," she said politely. "Though I'll miss the ghosts.''

He managed a wry smile. "Since you're the only one who's ever seen them, maybe they'll follow you.''

She shook her head. "You know they won't. They belong here."

You belong here, Katie. The words came into his head, spoken in his father's voice, and the sensation was so strong he shivered.

She was already gone, climbing the stone steps out of the gathering water, disappearing into the shadows. And he wouldn't call her back.

"I can't imagine how that door would have slammed shut," Mrs. Marvel was saying in her warm, comfortable voice.

"Neither can I." He glanced up into the darkness, almost thinking he could still see her, when an uneasy thought entered his brain. "Where's Willie?"

"You'll not be thinking he would have locked you in there?" Mrs. Marvel sounded like a mother lion defending her cub. "You know as well as I do that there's no harm in the boy. He wouldn't hurt a fly."

"Of course he wouldn't," O'Neal said swiftly. Wondering if he still believed it.

"The water must have pushed it closed," she said, starting up the stairs, her impressive bulk hiding any last sight of Katie's slim ankles.

"Yes," said O'Neal. It made perfect sense, one of life's little mysteries solved. But he didn't quite believe it.

"YOU TOLD ME you wanted to get rid of them," Willie said, his voice not much more than a whine. "I was just doing what you told me to do."

She slapped him, hard. "You didn't listen. Yes, they have to die. But not until I'm ready. We have to get rid of the girl first. Then things might calm down enough so that we can stay on for a bit longer. It's been peaceful here. We've got access to large sums of money that no one can trace. I'm not in any hurry to give that up."

"But you promised me..."

She slapped him again, and he didn't even flinch. "I promised you the girl. I said you could have her if you didn't take too much time with her. I didn't tell you it was O'Neal's time yet."

"But, Ma..."

"And by locking them in together, and sabotaging their lamp, you gave them the perfect chance. Did God take away your eyes as well as your brain, boy?"

"They don't like each other," he said with a snuffle.

"Idiot! They can't keep their eyes off each other. O'Neal's obsessed with her. It would be hysterically funny if it weren't so dangerous. He's been fighting it, but locking the two of them up isn't the way to keep them apart."

"She hates him. She's always arguing."

Mrs. Marvel snorted, giving up the notion of hitting him again. It did little good, and her hand was numb. "She's besotted, poor fool. He's a handsome man, and she's just silly enough to imagine herself in love with him. A dangerous combination if the two of them are thrown together. Which is exactly what happened when you were fool enough to lock them in the vault room."

"I don't see what it matters…"

"If he starts to care about her then he won't be willing to keep on with the comfortable life we've been living. If he knows she's dead he'll be in such a state he won't be bringing in any more money, and if he just thinks she's disappeared he'll probably go after her and leave us in peace."

"Sorry, ma," Willie muttered.

She slapped him again, just for good measure. "You try my patience, boy."

"I can go up now," he said eagerly. "Finish her off before anything else happens."

"No." She took a deep breath. "Things should be safe enough for the night. Unlike you, I have a brain in my head. Those two were up to something in the vault room, and now they regret it. They won't go anywhere near each other tonight. Tomorrow morning will be soon enough. Either the storm will be over, and you can drive her into town, or we'll dispose of her some other way."

"Drive her into town? But, Ma, you promised!"

"What's a poor mother to do?" Mrs. Marvel asked herself wearily. She looked back at her son. "Haven't you been listening to me? I don't mean *really* drive her into town. Just take her far enough away and do what you like.''

"Yes, Ma," Willie said happily.

THE ELECTRICITY lasted long enough for Katie to have a hot shower, change into the nightgown Mrs. Marvel had left her and crawl into bed, all set to discover whether she still loved Jane Austen as much as she used to. Not that the low-wattage bulb in her cavernous room would have done her eyesight much good, but the blackness that closed down around her was far too reminiscent of her sojourn in the water-soaked vault room, unpleasantly so.

This time she was alone, she thought. Thank God, of course. She would hardly want to be lying curled up in bed with O'Neal for company, now would she? Would she?

The wind had risen to a high-pitched shriek, battering against the windows, shaking them in their casings. O'Neal had said the storm would be over by morning. O'Neal had any number of strange notions.

One of his strangest had been to kiss her. She still wasn't quite sure why he had. He found her annoying, intrusive, smart-mouthed, all of which she admitted she was. Why in the world would he want to kiss her? Want to do even more than that? If Mrs. Marvel hadn't rescued them they would have ended up on that hard wooden counter with her dress up about her waist. Not the most romantic of fantasies, but she'd been beyond romance and over the edge into shivering passion.

They used to say that calories consumed alone didn't count. Did having sex in the pitch-dark count? Katie couldn't begin to guess, considering she'd never had sex in her entire twenty-eight years, which had to be some sort of record.

Her lifelong celibacy had begun accidentally. Even though her family had lapsed from the Mother Church, she'd seen *The Nun's Story* on television one Sunday afternoon and decided if she became a nun she'd get to wear wonderful, enveloping costumes and look just like Audrey Hepburn. She outgrew that notion in her teens, but the boys she grew up with had never seemed the slightest bit tempting. College was even worse—they were either jocks or nerds or idiots, and even if she started to like someone she never could bring herself to like them *that* much. And wouldn't you just know it, the first man she decided she did like that much turned out to be a bad-tempered hermit who had no interest in her.

Well, actually that wasn't strictly true. She could still feel the cool, strong touch of his hand between her breasts, pressed against her heart. She could taste his mouth, the strange, sorrowful possessiveness of it, and she'd wanted to drown in it. Drown in the darkness and his body, the feel of his hands sliding up her legs, knowing he could pull that dress from her and...

She kicked against the cover, furious with herself. She was being ridiculous, she who prided herself on her no-nonsense attitude. This place had a dangerous effect on her. She had gone from a hardheaded, practical young woman to a dreamy romantic, seeing ghosts, longing for a man who could give her absolutely nothing but trouble.

And the longer she stayed, the more enmeshed she became. With the ghosts. With him.

She tossed on the lumpy mattress, rolling over onto her stomach and glowering at her feather pillow in the darkness. It was almost as if this were an enchanted place. Led here by ghosts, watched over by a caretaker and her silent son, lured by a brooding master of the house worthy of a gothic romance, it was almost as if this place didn't really exist. The lack of outside communication, even with the car radio, and the determination of the elements to keep her here seemed almost supernatural.

Not to mention the ghosts.

But it wasn't the friendly spirits that occasionally appeared, apparently only to her, that she found so unsettling. It was O'Neal. O'Neal from a distance, glowering at her, watching her. O'Neal up close, touching her, kissing her. He was so cold, until she touched him, and then his skin would blaze with warmth. She wanted to warm him. She wanted to wrap her body around him and fill him with heat and life.

She had to be out of her mind.

She rolled over on her back again, peering into the darkness. There were candles and matches on the bedside table in case the unreliable electricity went out, but she made no effort to reach over and light it. There would be nothing to see, just the shifting shadows cast by the candle's glow, and she was already imagining enough hidden there in the darkness.

"Fiona." Her voice sounded unnaturally loud, even over the noise of the wind. "Fiona, are you there?"

Nothing moved in the room, no poltergeist tossed anything at her, no presence danced across the air to touch her. She'd felt those small, ghostly hands in her back, propelling her toward O'Neal, but she'd been too caught up in what had happened next to think about who or what had pushed her.

"Fiona, why did you push me at your brother?"

The room was silent. There were no ghosts there, listening. Maybe there never had been.

Katie sighed, wiggling down beneath the worn, ironed sheets. Whether she wanted to leave this place or not, she would. No matter how fierce the wind, no matter how driving the rain, she would damn well walk out of here tomorrow, rather than spend one more night being haunted. Not by the ghosts of O'Neal's drowned family.

But by O'Neal himself. And her crazy longing for him.

THE STEPS LED down to the sea. On a bright, cloudless day they led out onto a stretch of rocky beach where one could even launch a small curragh. But right now the water came halfway up the steps, and the waves surged even higher.

O'Neal paused halfway down those stone steps, letting the wind buffet him as he stripped off his clothes. He could feel the change coming over him, the darkness that called to him, and this time he would not resist it.

It was always his choice. Even years ago, the first time, when his family had been swept away from him and there was nothing he could do to save them, he'd felt the change and fought it, not even knowing what it was. He supposed he could have kept fighting and drowned, along with the others, but instead he'd eventually embraced the darkness, gone toward that pinprick of light and been transformed.

It was quite easy now, almost effortless due to long experience. He could shift back and forth quickly, even efficiently, and no one who watched would have any idea what they were seeing.

And if they saw, they wouldn't believe.

There were times he'd thought that Willie had watched him, hiding in the bushes, staring down at him as he moved from one life to another. But who would he tell, and who would believe him? Not even his doting mother would believe such a bizarre tale.

No, he was safe. He stared out over the furious waves. A creature could be dashed against the rocks, even a sea creature. It was a risk he needed to take. He dove off the steps, down, down into the icy blackness of the storm-tossed seas.

And when he hit water he was a seal.

Chapter Twelve

The room was bathed with the palest moonlight, and above them stars danced in the heavens. Even before she opened her eyes Katie knew that was impossible. The constant roar of the winds, the incessant rain still surrounded the old house, and there would be no moon visible, no stars to see.

She considered keeping her eyes closed. Whatever it was that filled the room with such a pearlescent glow would probably be unbelievable, and she'd seen more than enough ghosts in the past few days to last her a lifetime. Besides, she had to be dreaming. So why give in to it? Far easier to keep her eyes tightly shut and will sleep back around her like a feather comforter.

"I know you're awake." The voice was soft as a sigh, with the Irish in it as rich as a song.

Katie kept her eyes closed. "You aren't supposed to talk," she muttered. "You're just supposed to appear and disappear."

"And so I would, if you weren't so blessed thick

about the whole thing." There was no mistaking the annoyance in the young voice, and Katie couldn't stop herself. She let her eyes flutter open, then slammed them shut again.

"Go away," she said.

Dead silence. Which, Katie thought a moment later, was probably far too accurate a phrase. She opened one eye tentatively, but her visitor was still there.

"Stop fighting your destiny, Katie Flynn," the pale, wispy ghost of Fiona O'Neal said with all the sharp-tonged asperity of an elderly maiden aunt. "Open your eyes, sit up in your bed and listen to me, or I'll be forced to do something about it."

She did as she was told, reluctantly. Fiona was perched, cross-legged, at the foot of her high, huge bed, and the light seemed to emanate from her. She was like those glow-in-the-dark stars that children pasted to their ceilings—except there was no green tinge to her aura. She looked as if she were sitting directly on Katie's feet, and yet Katie could feel no pressure.

"What would you do?"

Fiona's pale, sweet face creased in thought. "I'm that tempted to throw a pillow at you. However, those things aren't worth the effort. It's very hard for me to make things move, or feel my presence. I'm not really here, you know."

"I know," Katie said dryly. "You're a figment of my imagination."

"I most certainly am not," Fiona retorted. "How could you have imagined me? I don't expect you've seen me anywhere else but here, have you?"

"Then why am I the only person who's seen you? And the others, for that matter?"

"Think about it, girl," Fiona said sternly, addressing someone more than ten years her senior. "There's a reason you're here, a reason you can see us when no one else can even feel our presence, no matter how hard we try to break through."

She didn't want to hear this, Katie thought. She really and truly didn't want to hear this.

"I'm leaving in the morning," she said abruptly.

Fiona's mocking laugh was as light as thistledown, and Katie wondered absently whether you could smack a ghost. "You're not going anywhere, and you know it. I led you here, and you followed. There's no turning back."

"I thought I was following a piece of laundry blown by the wind," she protested.

"And why would you be doing that? You have a habit of following stray pieces of laundry into the wind?" Fiona scoffed. "No, Katie, don't fool yourself. Things are difficult enough without you lying to yourself and me as well. I brought you here for Jamie."

"Jamie?"

"O'Neal. My big brother. The man who's far more haunted than you, even though he's never seen a ghost face to face. You're here to save him,

Katie. Save him from the demons that drive him, save him from those murderous bastards who'd cut your throat as soon as look at you. You're here to love him, and you're not leaving until…"

"Until?" Katie prompted.

"Until you really want to," Fiona admitted finally. "If you really, truly want to leave tomorrow then you'll be able to."

"You're going to tell me you're controlling this storm?" Katie scoffed.

"Certainly not. We have no power over the weather. It's a hurricane for sure, tearing up the east coast of this wild country, and you'll have a hard time making it to safety tomorrow if you're determined to go. But I don't think you are. I think you want to solve the mystery of O'Neal and Seal Point, don't you?"

"I'm curious," Katie admitted grudgingly.

"Curiosity killed the cat. Satisfaction brought him back." Fiona smiled a faint, feline smile.

"But that doesn't mean I'm here to love him," Katie said belatedly as Fiona's unbelievable words sank in. "I don't know where you got such a ridiculous idea. Your brother is the least lovable man I've ever met in my entire life, and I wouldn't touch him with a ten-foot pole. If he's troubled and I can do anything to help, I will, but there's a limit to how much I'm willing to sacrifice…"

She wouldn't have thought a ghost could smirk.

"Where did I get such a ridiculous idea?" she repeated. "Maybe in the basement vault."

Color flooded Katie's face. "You locked us in!"

Fiona shook her head, and her white-blond hair floated softly in the air. "I can't do that. It took all my strength to give you that little shove, and then I was gone. But at least I had a glimpse of the two of you before I faded." She fanned herself with her hand. "If you're not in love then you're a brazen creature."

Katie didn't bother arguing—there was no way she could win. "If you didn't lock us in, who did?"

"Ah," said Fiona. "Now you're showing the sense God gave you. There's something very wrong about this place, and it's not the three of us. We've done our poor best to protect him, but there's a limit to what we can do. We need your help."

"Protect him from what?"

"Willie Marvel and his evil mother."

"Don't be absurd! Mrs. Marvel is the sweetest, warmest, nicest woman you'd ever want to meet. Granted, her son is a bit spooky, but she's absolutely wonderful."

"I doubt her husband would agree, but since they killed him and buried the pieces all along the sea coast I'm afraid he's unable to tell you."

Katie was silenced only for a moment. "So how come he's not a ghost? Why doesn't he hang out with you?"

Fiona shrugged. "If there was rhyme or reason

to these things I've yet to discover it. We're here, he's not. You would think a murdered man would have a hard time resting in peace, but that doesn't seem to be the case. Whereas the three of us died peacefully and well...and yet we're left here to watch over Jamie and see him safe.''

''You died peacefully and well?''

''Let me tell you, Katie, that drowning's not a bad thing at all, if one must die. It's very peaceful, once you stop fighting.''

''I'll keep that in mind,'' she said dryly.

''God pray that you never have to learn it,'' Fiona said in a sober voice. She rose, floating across the room in her trailing garments. ''Come with me, Katie Flynn.''

Katie stayed where she was, beneath the thick cover of the down quilt. ''Where?''

''I want to show you something.''

''If you want to prove that the Marvels are evil I'd rather not know,'' she said faintly. ''I'm sure that even if they are homicidal maniacs they'd have no cause to hurt me...''

''Homicidal maniacs don't need cause,'' Fiona said impatiently. ''Haven't you learned that yet? Don't you watch television, girl?''

''Do you?''

She nodded vigorously, and her silken hair wafted in the night air. ''Mrs. Marvel has a satellite dish and a TV in her room. O'Neal doesn't know about it, of course, and since the storm hit she hasn't been able to get any reception, but in the past I've spent many an hour watching it with her. Mind you, she doesn't know I'm there.'' She smiled sweetly. ''I'm particularly fond of 'The X-Files.'''

''That does it,'' Katie said. ''I have to be dreaming this.''

''If you're dreaming this then there's no harm in coming with me, now is there?'' Fiona asked. She wasn't standing on the ground, Katie noticed absently. She was floating several inches above it.

''I could catch my death of cold.''

''The Marvels will kill you first. Mrs. Marvel promised Willie he could play with you before he finished you off. I saw what he did the last time.'' She shuddered, a strange sight in such a willowy apparition.

Katie wasn't going to believe her, any more than she was going to believe in this absurd dream. And if she truly were in a dream, then any incipient pneumonia would also be imaginary. She slid out of bed and onto the floor. ''And you didn't stop him?'' she said, reaching for the shawl that lay draped across the bed. It didn't provide much warmth, and her feet were freezing, but since it was a dream it could hardly matter.

''I couldn't,'' Fiona said, and there was a grim note in her voice. ''None of us could. I could only sit there and weep.''

A cold chill ran down Katie's back that had absolutely nothing to do with the temperature of the room. "You're scaring me," she said.

"Good." She held out her hand. It was a small hand, that of an adolescent girl, and the green-stoned ring glowed against her pale white skin.

"Can I touch you?" Katie asked, curious.

Fiona shook her head in sorrow. "No. You aren't even seeing me—I'm just a reflection of your other senses. But I'll lead you true, Katie Flynn. Follow me, and I'll show you a wonder the likes of which you've never seen."

"You'd be hard put to top three ghosts and a hurricane," Katie murmured, half to herself.

"But this has to do with the man you love."

"I don't love…!" she started, but Fiona interrupted blandly.

"The man you belong to. The man who belongs to you. We know about such things, and we're never wrong."

"Who's this we? Ghosts?" she countered irritably.

"No." Fiona was almost affronted. "The Irish. And you know it, as well, no matter how much you try to deny it. You took one look at Jamie and knew he was your destiny. You've been trying to escape ever since."

"Maybe I'm not in the mood to meet my destiny at this point in my life," Katie muttered.

"Whether you're in the mood or not has nothing to do with it," Fiona said sternly. "It happens when it happens, and it won't do you any good to keep fighting it like this. Follow me, and stop arguing. You're as bad as me father."

And Katie followed, wrapping the shawl tight around her.

The electric lights in the hallway were out, though Katie had no idea whether it was another blackout or if someone had simply turned them off. It didn't matter…Fiona's evanescent glow illuminated the darkness perfectly, and she followed behind her dutifully enough.

"Can't you do something about the cold?" she called ahead to her. "For a dream, this is too damned uncomfortable."

Fiona looked back, a mischievous expression on her face. "It's your dream," she said. "You make it warmer."

Katie muttered something uncomplimentary as she followed her ghostly flashlight. "Where exactly are we going?"

"To Jamie's room."

Katie came to a full stop. "No way. I'm not about to go traipsing into his bedroom in the middle of the night, dressed like this, and you can't make me do it!"

Fiona didn't bother to look back. "He's not there," she said. "And I wouldn't think a flannel nightgown and an old shawl could be called provocative."

"If he isn't there, why are we going there?"

"I want to show you something."

"Where has he gone on a night like this? What if he comes back while we're poking around in his room? He probably won't see you—he hasn't in fifteen years and I don't suppose he'll start now. He'll think I..." She let the words trail off. "He'll get the wrong impression."

"I'm not going to show you anything in his room," Fiona said patiently. "His balcony has the best view of the ocean. I want to show you something out there."

"It's pitch-black and the middle of a hurricane. I'm not going to be able to see a damned thing." She started walking anyway, since Fiona didn't seem ready to stop.

"'A damned thing,'" Fiona echoed thoughtfully. "I don't think so. At least, I hope not. It shouldn't be too late."

"Too late for what?"

"Too late for Jamie. Too late for all of us," Fiona said mournfully. She'd stopped outside O'Neal's door, the very door he'd slammed in Katie's face when he'd escorted her out of there earlier that day.

"I don't know what you're talking about," Katie said stubbornly.

"Open the door, please."

"I will not," Katie shot back. "I told you I'm not going in there. If you want to you can open the door yourself."

"No, I can't. Not without draining every ounce of energy from me, and then we'd accomplish nothing." She turned to Katie, and there was pleading in her huge, pale eyes. "Do this for me, Katie Flynn. Trust me on this one. Help me do what I can't do myself."

She couldn't resist. The doorknob was cool beneath her hand, and she half expected it to be locked, after her earlier transgression. But it turned easily enough, and the door swung open, and Katie held her breath, terrified that O'Neal would jump out of bed and demand to know what the hell she was doing there.

Fiona moved into the room, her halo of light illuminating the empty, unmade bed. The deserted room. Katie barely had time to breathe a sigh of relief before Fiona got to the French doors that led out onto the parapet.

"I don't think so," Katie muttered. "I'm not going out into that. I'll be blown over the edge in this wind."

The doors were rattling in the frames, and the wind had risen to an eerie pitch, like a woman wailing. Fiona turned to her.

"You won't be able to see that well from here," she said.

"What is it I'm supposed to see?"

"Come and look."

Katie bit her lip, oddly reluctant. She had no idea what she would see on the other side of the storm-battered glass, but whatever it was would most likely shock and horrify her. Was Fiona right about the Marvels, and had they stored their victims out there? Or would O'Neal be there, watching her, wondering what the hell she was doing in his bedroom again?

She approached cautiously. "What would happen if I touched you?" she asked.

Fiona kept staring out into the impenetrable darkness. "Nothing," she said. "It would feel like you were touching air. You could walk right through me and you would feel nothing."

"What about you? Would you feel anything?"

"No," she said. "It's been more than fifteen years since I've felt a human touch."

"I'm sorry." Katie's voice was soft.

Fiona turned then, smiling brightly, freely. "I've grown used to it. But I'm not about to stand by and watch my brother suffer the same fate. He's not past saving, but the time will come when there's nothing that can be done. Even if the Marvels don't murder him, he'll be dead to the world."

"I wish I knew what you were talking about." Katie came up beside her, and the pale glow Fiona cast spread over Katie's nightgown and illuminated her face.

"He blames himself for our deaths," Fiona said. "And until he lets go of that grief and shame he won't be able to live with himself. You can help him."

"How could he blame himself?"

"Because he lived and we died. And he goes out and courts death, teases it, to see if this time it will take him. But I don't want him to die, Katie. Even if it meant he would be with us, I don't want him to die. I want him to live and marry and have children. I want him to be happy. He needs someone to love him. Even more, he needs someone he can love."

"But I'm not that woman!"

"You are, and you know it," Fiona said simply. She turned back to the storm-blackened windowpane. "Look at him out there! Sooner or later he'll die, unless you convince him that he has something to live for."

Katie could see absolutely nothing at all, just the silver lash of the rain against the windows. All was blackness, the night, the storm, the fear in her heart. The light in the room grew imperceptibly dimmer, and Katie pressed her face against the glass, staring outward.

She could see the dark waves, higher than they'd been before, high enough to be seen from the parapet. The storm had grown unbelievably intense, a nightmare of screaming wind and rain. "There's no one out there," she whispered, more a prayer, a hope, than a belief.

"Look in the ocean," Fiona said. It was almost pitch-black now, and she knew that if she looked beside her she wouldn't see Fiona at all. She could only hear her soft, plaintive voice. "Look out in the darkness, look with your eyes and look with your heart."

Katie looked. For a moment she thought she saw him, and she let out a strangled gasp before she realized that it wasn't O'Neal's dark head bobbing up and down in the teeming waves. It was the seal.

As always when she saw him, she felt that strange sense of peace and knowledge settle down over her. And a rare, deep fear that burned in her heart.

"He'll drown," she whispered, pain and fear in her voice.

"You see him?"

Katie turned her head. She could barely see Fiona in the darkness—only her eyes still glowed, rather like the Cheshire Cat in Alice in Wonderland. "No," she said. "I see the seal."

She could see Fiona's smile, as well, then, and the cat image was even more forcibly in her mind. "You see Jamie."

"I see…" The seal was motionless in the churning water, staring up at the parapet. There was no way he could see her, no way he could know she was there. No way that it would make any difference to an aquatic mammal without the sense to stay ashore during a bad storm.

But he looked at her. Across the torrent of ocean, his eyes were staring into hers.

"You see him," Fiona murmured, "and you

can't believe. But it's true, and deep in your heart you know it to be true. O'Neal is out there in the water. Watching you.''

"It's the seal," Katie protested uselessly.

"It's O'Neal. And you know it. Deep in your heart.''

And Katie did.

can't believe. But it's true, and deep in your heart you *know* it to be true. O'Neal is out there in the night. Waiting for us."

"It's insane," Jane protested uneasily.

"Yes, O'Neal. And you know it. Deep in your heart."

And Jane did.

Chapter Thirteen

She stood alone in the darkness, waiting for him. Fiona had left her, hours ago, it seemed, and the storm had grown wilder still. She could no longer see beyond the parapet to the ocean, she could no longer see the parapet itself, but still she stood there by the French doors, staring out into the darkness, waiting.

He might be dead, of course. She knew this with the last trace of reason that existed, but her life had been taken over by the unbelievable, and reason seemed far more remote than fantasy. Any creature, man or beast, who swam in that wild ocean took the risk of being dashed to pieces against the rocks. Why should O'Neal be any different? He was courting Death out there. What if Death decided to respond to O'Neal's advances and take him?

But she knew he'd come back. She could feel it in her heart as it lay beating steadily against the thick flannel of her borrowed nightgown. She could feel it in the warmth of her skin, in the pulse of her blood, in the marrow of her bones. He would come back from the sea. And she would be waiting for him.

She lost track of time. Her always-reliable watch had stopped, and there were no clocks in this house. No doleful grandfather clock chiming the hour, no sense of the passage of time. She was adrift in a calmer, timeless sea, waiting for him.

There was no lightening of the storm-blackened sky when he came, but she knew it was close to dawn. The door opened into the darkness and he stood there.

"What are you still doing here?" His voice was low, barely audible above the howl of the wind. She turned and leaned back against the glass door, feeling the storm shake behind her. She could only see his silhouette against the open door.

"How did you know I was in your room?"

"I saw you."

She wasn't expecting an honest answer. "Where were you when you saw me?"

There was a sudden flare of light as he lit a match, leaning over to light the candle on the table by his bed. It illuminated him harshly, throwing strange shadows around the room. He was wearing a pair of jeans and nothing else, and he was glistening with water. His long hair was pushed back, his eyes hooded as he turned to look at her.

She wanted to look away, but she couldn't. He was starkly beautiful in the wavering candlelight, mesmerizingly so. Frighteningly so, and she should have run away hours ago instead of waiting for him like a virgin sacrifice.

"Why are you here, Katie?" His voice was harsh. "Did you decide to have mercy on me and get in bed with me?"

"Who's being merciful?" she whispered.

He closed his eyes for a moment, as if he were in pain. "I'm not what you think I am," he said. "Go away, for God's sake. Go now!"

She took a step toward him, reacting to his pain rather than his rejection. "Jamie…" she said.

He recoiled as if he'd been slapped, and she stopped, halfway across the room.

"What did you call me?"

"Jamie," she said. "That's your name, isn't it?"

"No one here knows it. No one's called me by that name since my family died. How did you hear it?" There was no missing the grief and rage in his voice, and Katie wondered whether she should be frightened. "Did you go through all my papers until you found out everything you could? It couldn't have been very interesting reading. There are no scandals, I'm a legal immigrant to this country, and I have almost no business dealings with anyone. I just want to be left alone, by everyone, but most especially by you."

It couldn't have been clearer. Katie straightened her back, calling on her shredded dignity and telling herself she should welcome her escape. "Then I won't bother you any longer," she said, wrapping the shawl more tightly around her suddenly chilled body and starting for the door.

He made no move to stop her, when she was half-certain he would. He waited until she reached the door, then spoke.

"You didn't answer me. How did you know my name?"

Something inside her snapped. Some wild, angry part that responded to the call of the wind, the call of her tightly bound heart. "Your sister did, you stupid creature!" she shouted at him. "Your sister told me you needed me, and like a fool I listened. After all, I haven't much experience with ghosts— how was I to know she was out of her mind? You don't need anyone but the damned ocean and your solitude."

"You're mad," he said, his voice rich with disbelief. "Or prone to sleepwalking and nightmares."

Enough was enough. She spun on her heel and started toward him, fury shaking her body. She came right up to him and poked him, hard, in the chest. "Nightmare indeed," she said. "It's been a nightmare and a half since I've been here, *Jamie*," she said bitterly. "Ghosts and murderers and you glooming around like a tortured poet. I'm tired of this place and I'm mortally tired of you." She was about to poke him again, hard, when he caught her hand in his, stopping her.

He was cold, wet. He smelled of rain, not the

sea, and he needed to be warmed. "What murderers?" he asked in a suddenly patient voice.

"The Marvels. Your sister seems to believe Mrs. Marvel is an archcriminal."

She expected his usual contempt. Instead he was holding her hand, looking down at her with an odd expression on his face. "Don't call her that," he said in a hushed voice.

"Don't call Mrs. Marvel a murderer? I'm sure it's just part of my hallucinations...."

"Don't talk about my sister. She's not here, she's dead," he said.

"I know she's dead. But she's here. How else would I know your name?"

"I don't know," he said. His icy cold hands were starting to warm against her skin. He shut his eyes for a moment, his beautiful, extraordinary eyes. "Why are you here?" he asked her again. "Are you here to sleep with me?"

She wanted to pull her hand away from his, but she couldn't. He was holding it tightly, waiting for her answer. She knew what it should be. The answer she gave everyone—the clever, pat answer that neither wounded nor encouraged.

But this time she couldn't give it. This time she couldn't pull away. Every other time in her life, when it looked as if she was headed into bed with someone, she would stop, because it just didn't feel right.

And now, of all places, with all people, it felt right.

But she'd be damned before she'd admit it.

"I'm going back to my room," she said. Making no effort to extricate herself from his grasp.

"I want you, you know," he said, and he sounded half-surprised at himself. "I've wanted you since I first saw you, sitting like an idiot in that car perched halfway over the cliffs. I watch you when you aren't looking. I dream about you, long, lush, erotic dreams. I think about what your body would look like. Feel like. Taste like."

Heat flooded her, and she fought it, fought the drugging pleasure of his words. "Anyone would look good to a hermit," she said, tugging at her hand. "Believe me, you'd be vastly disappointed with reality."

"I don't spend my entire life here, you know. I go out, to Boston, to New York, to Dublin. I flirt with beautiful women, and occasionally I sleep with them. I'm not a desperate man."

She looked up at him. "Aren't you?" she whispered.

His wry smile was heartbreaking. "That's the problem with you. You see me far too clearly. I am desperate. But not for sex. I'm desperate for you, Katie Flynn. For you."

Somehow her fist had uncurled in his grasp, and her hand was spread out against his chest, against the warm, smooth skin. She wanted to reach up her other hand, as well, to touch him, but she kept it balled in a fist by her side. Fear was coursing through her now. Fear of the inevitable, fear of the unknown.

"I don't do this," she said helplessly, she who was never helpless, always strong.

"Don't do what? Go to bed with men you've just met? You always wait until you've built up a long-term relationship?" His voice was lightly mocking, and he caught her other hand in his, uncurling that fist as well.

"No," she said. "I don't have sex with anyone. Ever."

She'd half hoped she would startle him into dropping her hands, leaving her alone. He didn't. He didn't even seem particularly surprised, as if he'd somehow guessed how inexperienced she actually was. "Then why are you going to sleep with me?"

"I'm not going to. I'm going back to my room and back to sleep, and when it's daylight I'll find my way out of here..."

"Stop talking," he said gently. "Unless you're going to tell me the truth."

It was his eyes that seduced her. If he'd kept them closed she might have had a chance. But those beautiful, tormented eyes ate into her soul, and she looked up into them and knew she no longer had any choice. She'd made her decision, whether she regretted it or not.

"All right," she said. "Why? Maybe because

you need me. But other men have needed me. Because you're beautiful? I'm not someone who puts great store in physical beauty. Because I want you? I've wanted other men.''

"Then why haven't you slept with them?"

"Because it didn't feel right." The words were out of her mouth before she could call them back.

"You don't think you're in love with me, do you?" He sounded almost distant, reaching up a hand to gently touch the side of her face. She let him, leaning against him.

"No," she said. "I don't think I'm in love with you." The truth was stark, shattering and undeniable. She didn't think she was in love with him. She knew it. In less than two days she'd fallen in love with a mystery. For the first time in her life she'd done something impulsive, impractical, and life altering. And she was about to act upon it as well.

He reached up with his other hand, cupping her face and staring down at her with his dark, beautiful eyes. She wondered if he knew the truth. She almost hoped he did. "Then why are you going to let me make love to you, *macushla?*"

She was the one who closed her eyes, no longer able to look at him. "Because if you don't," she said in a whisper, "I think I might die."

His mouth was feather soft, brushing against hers. It was a kiss like no other kiss, one of tenderness and blessing, a chaste kiss, promising carnal pleasures.

She could feel his heartbeat beneath her hand, and she sighed against his mouth, wanting more.

He kissed her closed eyelids, he kissed her brow and the corners of her eyes. He tilted her face up to his and kissed her trembling lips, slowly deepening it, and she welcomed the hot, damp possession of his mouth on hers, welcomed the gathering darkness.

She slid her hands up his cool, smooth chest, and his flesh warmed to her touch. When she reached his shoulders she clung to him. Outside, the storm raged; inside, she was buffeted by emotions stronger than any gale force winds.

He must have sensed her unexpected weakness. He scooped her up in his arms effortlessly, and she'd forgotten how strong he was. Kicking the door shut, he carried her to the bed, settling her down against the softness of the rumpled sheets.

"Blow out the candle," she whispered.

"Why? Do you think the ghosts will want to watch?" He stood over her, the flame throwing eerie shadows around him. She felt vulnerable, frightened, and the web of erotic enchantment spread over her, trapping her on the mattress. And she had no real wish to escape.

He knelt beside her, looming over her, and she knew escape was out of the question. "I want to see you,'' he said, reaching up to unfasten the buttons at her throat. ''I want to watch you.''

''I'm frightened,'' she said.

''I know.''

There were only three buttons. The voluminous night gown wrapped around her like a shroud. ''Where did this come from?'' he asked.

''I assume it belongs to Mrs. Marvel,'' she replied nervously.

The sudden sound of tearing material was shocking in the room, as he ripped the nightgown open from neck to hem. The flannel was old, soft and weak, and it tore easily enough. She resisted the almost overwhelming need to pull the torn pieces back around her, forcing her hands to lie flat against the bed.

He sat back, his beautiful eyes hooded as they ran the length of her body. And then he leaned forward and placed a kiss on her collarbone, carefully moving the torn nightgown out of the way.

He moved slowly down her body, lightly kissing each part of her skin as he exposed it, and the feel of his mouth was like fire. Every move was deliberate, careful not to frighten her, but the heat of his mouth was stirring her blood to a boiling point, and she needed him to touch her, take her.

She kept thinking she would fall into a romantic stupor, where time and action would become some sort of dream, but everything was sharply clear. The feel of his cool, strong hands as they covered her breasts, the wet tug of his mouth as he suckled her. When he stripped off his jeans and lay beside her on the bed, she was acutely aware of his hands sliding between her legs, pulling them apart. Touching her. Her fierce jolt of response when he touched her was a shock, and then she was past surprise and soaring over into sheer sensation, as his fingers slid deep inside her.

She couldn't catch her breath. His long damp hair was all around them, and she felt as if she were in a vast ocean of endless desire. She reached out for him, and she whispered something, she wasn't sure what. It might have been "please." It might have been "love."

He moved between her legs, leaning over her, and she told herself she wasn't afraid.

"Hold on to me," he whispered against her ear. "Hold on tight."

She put her hands on his shoulders, and she could feel him against her, hot and heavy, pressing, filling her, sliding in a little at a time, and then withdrawing, only to push inside her again, deeper this time.

Her fingernails were digging into his shoulders now, but he didn't seem to mind. He rocked against her, a slow, leisurely pace that was maddening when she needed more, she needed all of him, not this wicked tease, this promise of something shattering and unattainable.

"Please," she said again, this time knowing what she was asking for. She arched her hips, trying to pull him in deeper, but he simply caught and held her, moving in and out, deeper and yet not deep enough, his pace swift, taunting, impossibly arousing.

She was wet, sleek and needy, and she clawed at him, desperate. Her body was iron hard with tension, and he was covered with sweat, and still he wouldn't finish it, still he teased to the point of madness.

"Look at me, Katie," he said in a harsh voice. She opened her eyes, staring up into his lost, beautiful ones. Her breath and her heart stopped as he thrust deep, breaking past the barrier of her virginity and filling her completely.

The pain was nothing, the joy powerful. She no longer clawed his skin, she slid her arms around his neck and kissed him with pure abandon and love.

She was unprepared for the spiral of dark pleasure that moved within her as he rocked against her. He put his hands under her and pulled her up to meet his thrusts, and she could feel tears running down her face and she couldn't begin to guess why. He moved faster now, harder, and she wrapped her legs high around him, all of her life centered around the joining of their bodies, pulsing, surging together.

The first tremor that washed over her was a surprise, the second a shock. The third was so profound she found herself spinning out of control, convulsing in a deathlike dream with his body all around her, inside her, filling her with life and hot, wet desire.

She was crying, she realized belatedly. Sobbing, but O'Neal didn't seem to mind. He rolled to his side, taking her with him, holding her with all the tenderness of a lover.

He was her lover, she thought in amazement, weeping her stupid tears against his chest while he stroked her hair and murmured soft, loving things that made no sense. He was her lover and her love.

And she fell asleep mid-sob.

HE DIDN'T EVEN WANT to think about how big a mistake he'd made in taking Katie Flynn to bed with him. She lay sleeping in his arms, exhausted by sex and tears, and if he had any sense at all he'd pull away from her, toss a down comforter around her and make himself scarce.

If he simply disappeared she'd have no choice but to leave, without seeing him again. It would be hard for her, but not as hard as facing reality. Not as painful as realizing she'd made love with a creature not quite human.

Of course he'd known he should never touch her. Each time he had, the need for her had grown, so that he'd been in a state of desperation after their sojourn in the flooded vault room, when he'd tasted her mouth, her skin, breathed in her longing for him. A longing that almost matched his own.

He needed her. It was that simple, and that damning. He'd spent the last fifteen years making certain he needed absolutely nothing and no one. And then Katie Flynn had shown up like some orphan from the storm, and he'd been doomed. He'd tried to warn her away. He'd been rude, condescending, overbearing and taciturn.

And she had simply laughed at him. Ignored his moods. And made him fall in love with her, when a few days ago he would have said that was an impossibility. That he'd lost the ability to love.

You can't fall in love in three days, he knew that simple fact far too well. He doubted even the existence of love.

But his common sense had been no defense at all against an Irish waif who looked at him with eyes far too wise for her years. A creature who saw ghosts and talked to them and came to his room and handed over her virginity after twenty-some years of saving it.

There was no way he could change things. No way he could be anything else than what he was. Half man, half creature, doomed to live in solitude. Taking comfort in Katie Flynn's arms had been the most disrupting thing he could do. He would never find peace again.

The ocean wouldn't have him, no matter how many times he offered himself. He was doomed, but he didn't have to doom her, as well. She was too young, too full of life to share the darkness that covered him. Once she escaped this place there'd be no more ghosts for her. Only a faint memory of her first lover.

If he stayed in bed with her he would take her again. And again, every way he could think of. From the back, up against the wall, with his mouth, with his heart.

He couldn't risk it. He'd gone too far to save himself. But one act of love wouldn't have to destroy her, too. She might not even think it was love.

But he knew it was. And that would be one more nail in his coffin. One more piece of eternal damnation.

And he slid out of her arms, out of the bed. Out of her life.

And disappeared into the night.

Chapter Fourteen

The room was still dark when she awoke, sticky, achy, alone. She had no illusions that it was still night. Unbelievably the storm seemed to have grown stronger still, the wind a constant wail beyond the glass doors. She sat up in his bed, pulling a sheet around her, and wondered where he was. And why he hadn't stayed with her.

There were a thousand obvious answers to that. He'd had what he wanted, and when he was finished there was no reason to stay. Except that Katie had no illusions about her appeal as a femme fatale, and she doubted O'Neal had simply been overcome by unstoppable lust when he'd taken her to bed. O'Neal was a man in fierce control of his life, his emotions and undoubtedly his hormones, as well.

She only wished she could say the same for herself.

She'd made a mess of things, that was for sure. After years of resisting some of the most eligible, charming men of her acquaintance, she'd fallen stupidly, hopelessly in love with a creature—

A sudden vision returned to her, of the seal, arcing through the waves, graceful, powerful against the fierce surf. She could hear Fiona's voice in her head, whispering. *You can't believe it, it makes no sense.*

It still made no sense to her, but she was past the point of dwelling on it. Last night she'd been bewitched, haunted, caught up in an enchantment. Today she was ready to face the consequences. And face O'Neal.

There was one major problem with having your clothes ripped from you in a moment of passion, she decided a few minutes later. What the hell did you wear when it was time to go back to your own room? Mrs. Marvel's flannel nightgown was in tatters, ripped down the middle. Instead Katie pulled the sheet from the bed and wrapped it around herself, toga-style. It was still early enough that she was unlikely to meet anyone in the corridors. As far as she knew, the Marvels seldom ventured above stairs. And she had the strong suspicion that O'Neal would be keeping his distance, if he had anything to say in the matter.

He didn't.

The hallway was cool and deserted, and she made it back to her own room safely enough. She had no idea how the water system worked in this place, and whether it would work with the power being out for so long, but she didn't care. She was going to get clean if she had to hang herself out a window in the storm.

There was water in the shower that was slightly warm. She bathed quickly, finishing just before it slowed to an icy trickle, and wrapped herself in a thick towel. The bathroom was dark. The window was an impenetrable sheet of gray water. Katie peered at her reflection in the mirror, wondering if she'd look different. If anyone could look at her and see that her life had changed. Did she look wanton? Did she look lost?

She dressed quickly in her own clothes this time, absurdly grateful for the familiar feel of baggy jeans and cotton sweater. She had a miserable headache, probably from lack of caffeine, and she was absolutely ravenous. Maybe Mrs. Marvel had cooked muffins again.

Another memory came to her, sharp and acrid like the stink of toxic waste. Fiona had called the Marvels murderers.

For heaven's sake, the ghost of Fiona O'Neal had told her that O'Neal himself was some sort of bewitched creature who could change himself into a seal. Surely she wasn't going to start believing in weird hallucinations like those?

"Fiona?" she said out loud. There was no answer. In truth, the O'Neal family were not very convenient ghosts. They were never there when you needed them.

"What in God's name have you done to me?" Katie murmured out loud.

There were no such things as ghosts or seal people or cozy housekeepers hiding a murderous streak. There was only one twenty-eight-year-old former virgin who had a far-too-active imagination.

"There's nothing wrong here," she said out loud. "Nothing that a little sunshine and common sense wouldn't fix."

The tree limb crashed through her window, shattering the glass and the mullions and skittering across the floor like a guided weapon. Katie was so shocked she couldn't move, could only stand there and watch it fly toward her with deadly intent.

She wasn't even aware that it had stopped a few feet short of her. The wind howled through the broken glass like a hungry demon, whipping everything up, catching Katie's wet hair and lashing it against her face, pulling at her clothes, tugging at her. She ran from the room, slamming the door after her, but the sound of the angry wind followed her, chasing her down the dark, deserted hallways.

The kitchen was empty, cold and lifeless. There was no coffee on the stove, no fresh muffins, no sign of Mrs. Marvel. It was after ten in the morning—the battery-powered clock on the wall told her that much, but clearly Mrs. Marvel hadn't entered the kitchen that morning.

First things first, Katie thought, rummaging in the darkened refrigerator for something edible. She settled for some cheese and a bottle of flat cola, desperate for any form of caffeine, before she turned to face the mess she was in. Her first thought was the network of cellars. Had the water risen so high that the entire house might go? Were Mrs. Marvel and her son down there, trying to stop the inexorable rise of the sea? Or had they drowned in the basement, trapped by the storm?

There were no flashlights in the kitchen, only a few candle stubs, but she lit one, taking it with her to the basement stairs, holding her breath and saying a silent prayer before she opened the door, holding the meager light over her head to illuminate the black passageway.

The smell of the sea was overpoweringly strong. She could hear the water beneath, lapping against the stone, though she couldn't see how far it had risen. She took a tentative step forward, peering into the darkness.

"Is there anyone down there?" she called. "Mrs. Marvel? O'Neal?"

"They're not there, miss."

Willie's slow, deep voice came from directly behind her. She shrieked, startled, and the wax from the candle splashed onto her hand. She dropped it, and it went out, rolling down the stairs into the darkness, landing with a splash in the gathering water.

They were in darkness, the two of them. In the murky light she could just see his huge form blocking the doorway, blocking the exit. There was nowhere else she could go. Below her lay the flooded passageways, vaults and cellars. Above her stood Willie.

She didn't move. She had no real reason to be afraid of him, only a dream conversation with a ghost, only a sense of uneasiness that had no connection to reality. She took a deep breath, trying to calm herself.

"Where are they, Willie?"

"O'Neal's out there in the storm. He won't hear a thing—the wind is making too much noise. It sounds like a woman screaming, doesn't it?"

Her entire body felt suddenly cold and clammy. "Yes, it does," she said, keeping her voice calm. "Where's your mother? You know she told you to look after me. She wouldn't like it if something happened to me."

The slow, soft chuckle was the most terrifying sound of all. "I'm looking after you, miss. Just the way she told me to. She said I could do anything I want with you, as long as I didn't make too much of a mess. And as long as O'Neal wasn't around."

"Why would that matter?"

Willie snorted. "I'm not stupid, you know. I have eyes in my head. I know the way he looks at you. I know the dirty things you do when you think no one's around."

"Were you watching us, Willie?" she asked calmly, edging down a step.

"I don't need to watch. I know what people do. Dirty things, and you're dirty, too. Disgusting. You know what he is, don't you? I know you do. Ma won't believe me when I try to tell her. She hits me and tells me not to make up stories, but I've seen him change. He turns into a seal, and he dives down and brings up treasures from the bottom of the ocean. That's where all the money comes from."

"Very clever, Willie," she said softly. Another step down. Dampness was seeping into her sneakers, but she couldn't afford to let that stop her. If she had to she could swim for it.

"How could you let a creature like that touch you?" he demanded mournfully.

"I don't know, Willie." She pitched her voice a little higher as she took another step down, away from him, into ankle-deep water, hoping he wouldn't notice she was moving farther and farther away. "What did you want to do with me?"

"I want to kill you," he said simply. "That's all. I like to hurt things, and see how they cry. How long it takes them to die. You're in the way, you know. If you'd been able to leave yesterday then things would have been all right. O'Neal would have forgotten about you. But you stayed too long, and now I have to punish you."

"I couldn't leave. The storm was too powerful."

"Too bad for you," Willie said. "There's no way out, you know. The cellars are flooded."

She took another step down, and the water was almost to her knees. It was icy, icy cold, and she wondered how long she could last down there. Fiona had promised her that drowning was an easy death. Maybe she was about to find out. She would rather drown than let Willie get his hands on her.

"Don't make me come down there after you," he warned her in his soft voice. "I don't like it in the dark. There are things down there."

She paused. "What things, Willie? Ghosts?"

"I don't believe in ghosts. Ma says such things don't exist," he said flatly. "I know she's right. If there were ghosts then I would have seen them. That girl from Portland would come back, and the two boys down in Camden. And my father."

"You killed your father, Willie?"

Wrong question. "Don't say anything about my father!" he shrieked, throwing himself down the stairs after her.

She made a dive for the water, but she wasn't fast enough. His thick hand caught her arm and hauled her out of the water. She stared up at him in the darkness, too stunned to struggle. He was breathing through his mouth, deep, panicked breaths, and she thought she could see the faint gleam of madness in his eyes. It was probably her imagination—it was too dark to see anything. She only knew that his eyes would be mad.

"Where's your mother, Willie?" she asked

again, desperate. "Does she know you killed your father? Does she know you hurt people?"

"She told me to kill him. She said he wanted to send me away." His voice was soft, almost confused. "I have to do what my ma tells me, don't I?"

"Not always, Willie. You don't really want to hurt me, do you? Wouldn't you rather let me go?"

"No."

"But why, Willie? What have I ever done to you?"

"You talk to the ghosts. I don't like that. I don't like people pretending they can see ghosts. When people are dead, they're dead. They don't come back to haunt you. You won't come back, either. You'll be gone, just like the rest of them, and no one will even find what's left of your body."

It was the last straw. She panicked, kicking at him, but she might as well have been kicking a brick wall. He took no notice of her struggles, simply wrapping his big hands around her and hauling her up the darkened stairs.

She screamed when they got to the top, and he shoved her against the wall and hit her, hard, knocking her into dazed silence before he threw her over his shoulder and started toward the stairs.

She clawed at the banister, but he simply yanked her free, slamming her against the stone wall as he mounted the stairs. He seemed impervious to her fists beating at his back, her useless attempts to kick him, and she'd just about given up hope when he stopped, utterly still, on the landing at the top of the wide stone staircase.

There was a faint glow coming from somewhere in front of them, but from her position slung over his shoulder she couldn't see its source. All she could sense was the sudden terror that stiffened Willie's huge body.

His tight grip on her slackened, and with a jerk she slid down, away from him, landing in a heap at his feet, too dazed to scramble away. He was staring straight ahead, no longer even aware of her presence, and she turned to follow his gaze.

The old man stood there, his red hair on end, his mouth an empty *O* of fury, as he pointed a pale, glowing hand at Willie. "Murderer," Da intoned in an awful voice. "Vile, cruel beast."

Willie was shaking all over in abject terror and frustrated rage. Obviously someone else could finally see and hear the ghosts of O'Neal's family. "I don't believe in you," he said in a harsh voice. "I don't know you. You can't be haunting me..."

"I'm haunting you, lad!" Da thundered, his sepulchral voice carrying over the noise of the storm. "I know the things you've done. And I'm here to punish you for your sins. You touch that girl again, and I'll show you such horror you'll be struck blind and dumb."

Katie started to edge away. Bad move, she thought. Willie had almost forgotten about her existence, but at Da's words he looked down at her, his frightened eyes narrowing in sudden cunning. "Come any closer to me and I'll throw her over the side," he said, reaching down for her.

"Noooooo!" From out of the darkness came the woman, shrieking like an ancestral banshee as she rushed toward him, a pale orange glow around her. It was too much for Willie. With a hoarse scream he held up his hands to ward her off and stumbled backward. Down the long, winding stone steps.

It took forever for him to end his fall. The sound of snapping bones echoed eerily in the cavernous hallway, and the sudden silence was awful.

"Is he dead then, love?" Da asked in a pleasant voice.

The woman leaned over the balcony, staring down at the figure sprawled at an awkward angle, blood pooling beneath his smashed skull. "Thoroughly dead, my dear," she said, her voice as Irish as his.

"Damn, but I enjoyed that, Maeve," he said. "Nasty little piece of goods, that Willie. Wish we'd done something about him years ago."

"We couldn't." She turned to Katie, who still sat huddled on the stairs, listening to their conversation in dull amazement. Maybe Willie had hit her harder than she thought. She must have fallen. These two luminous creatures couldn't really be standing—no, floating there, looking at her with such knowing eyes.

"She knows why she's here, doesn't she?" Maeve asked her husband. "Fiona's able to talk to her, isn't she?"

"I think she hears us as well, love," Da said. "Don't you, lass?"

Katie just stared at him.

"You've gone and scared the girl witless," Maeve scolded him. "She's seen you before, though I don't expect she can understand a word you're saying."

"Where's Fiona?"

"Watching over her brother, of course. Not that he can see her, the stubborn boy. She's afraid he's going to throw himself into the sea out of guilt."

"Guilt? What's the lad to feel guilty about?"

Maeve cast a speaking glance at Katie. "I don't think they spent last night playing cards, dearest."

"Then he'll have to marry the girl. That's what we wanted, isn't it? She's the right one. Otherwise she wouldn't be able to see us."

"She's the right one. I'm just not sure if she knows it herself."

"She knows it herself," Katie said in a firm voice, rising on unsteady feet.

"I told you she could hear us," Da said triumphantly.

"Where is O'Neal?"

"Jamie? He's out somewhere, and Fiona's having a devil of a time keeping up with him. Go after them, lass. Find your man and take him.''

"Seamus!" Maeve said in shocked tones.

"Take him in holy matrimony," Da amended sheepishly. "He'll have you. We brought the boy up right, and he's half-mad over you as it is. But mind the old lady. She's around here somewhere, and I don't know how much help we can be. She's no fool like her son, easily frightened by a pair of shades. I doubt she could even see us.''

"What do you mean? Can't you make her see you?''

Da shook his head. "A dark soul like hers can see no light. She won't like finding her son dead. She won't mourn, but she'll be in a royal snit.''

"Seamus." Maeve's voice was softly reproving.

"She's a dangerous creature, and I'm not sure Jamie knows it. Go after him, lass. Love him. And keep him safe.''

They were gone. That quickly, the two of them vanished, and she was alone in the cold, dark hallway. Alone with the corpse of the man who tried to kill her.

Her knees were wobbly, her head ached, her jaw throbbed, and she had to cling very tightly to the smoothly carved wooden banister as she made her way down the stairs. Willie lay on the floor at her feet, and there was no doubt he was thoroughly dead. His sightless eyes stared upward, his slack mouth hung open, and he lay surrounded by a halo of blood.

She stared at him in numb horror, half waiting for him to sit up, to come after her, dead or not. But Willie didn't move. He was gone, and he'd left no ghost behind to finish his filthy business.

She couldn't open the front door. At first she thought it was locked, then she realized the force of the wind was holding it closed. She struggled, but she was no match for the fury of the winds. She needed to find O'Neal, needed him with a desperation that tore at her heart. She ran back to the library, ignoring the body that lay in the hall, ran to the tall windows that overlooked the lawn. She picked up the nearest chair and flung it through the casement window, shattering the glass. The wind speared through the broken panes, but she ignored it, smashed against it with the iron fire poker until she made a space large enough for her to climb out into the heart of the storm.

The wind fought her, crazily, and she could barely force herself through the empty casement. She landed on her hands and knees beneath the window, and shards of glass cut through her jeans. She staggered to her feet, barely able to stand in the screaming winds, and called out his name.

"Jamie!" The sound was whipped away from her, carried up to the heavens, and there was no way he could hear her. He could be anywhere in this storm, he could have retreated once more to the churning ocean, courting death. She had to find him. If he wanted her gone, she would leave, but she had to see him, touch him, just once more.

The wind sounds like a woman screaming. Willie had said that, and the words haunted her, as the sound of a shrill, keening sound rose into the storm. And Katie knew with sudden horror that Mrs. Marvel had found her son.

Chapter Fifteen

It took Katie less than a minute to realize that she may have made a very grave mistake. Each time she tried to rise to her feet the wind smashed her down again, tearing at her like a thousand angry harpies, screaming at her. The best she could manage was to crawl on her hands and knees through the mud and bracken, keeping low so the wind couldn't catch her and toss her in its angry grip.

There were trees down everywhere, littering the expanse of lawn that led to the cliffs, leaning against the mansion, knocking through windows. The rain was blinding, beating down painfully, and the ground beneath Katie's hands and knees was a wash of mud.

She had no idea where she wanted to go, where she could go, for shelter, for safety. Even more important, where she could find O'Neal. She didn't have much choice. She crouched low to the ground, keeping in close to the side of the building as she worked her way around it, clinging blindly to anything her numb wet hands could find.

It seemed to take forever for her to reach the fortresslike front of the house. The courtyard was flooded with several inches of muddy water, but the stone walls provided some respite from the howling winds, and she managed to pull herself to her feet.

She tried screaming his name, but the howl of the storm drowned her out, and she gave up the effort, instead concentrating on finding shelter. If O'Neal had any sense at all he'd be someplace reasonably warm and dry, as well, and it shouldn't take her long to find him.

If O'Neal had any sense.

She no longer even thought about how uncomfortable she was. Her clothes were soaked with the cold, driving rain, her sneakers saturated from her attempt at escape. Her hands were numb with the cold—she could see the blood from a dozen tiny cuts being washed away by the ceaseless rain, but she viewed it dispassionately.

She had two choices. The stables that now served as a garage were nearby. Willie wouldn't be there, Willie was gone forever, and she might find safety despite the rising water. They were on a high spit of land—there was no way the storm tide could rise enough to flood the old mansion. She could curl up in the back of one of the cars and wait out the storm, wait out Mrs. Marvel's murderous wrath, in relative warmth and safety.

Or there was the guest house. She could barely see its outline against the silver-black rain. It stood on lower ground, it was made of wood and stone, and there was no way it could be as secure as the huge stone mansion.

And yet it called to her. Warmth and safety, shelter from the storm. Was O'Neal there?

Don't be daft. The voice in her head was Da's, rich with asperity. *He'll have checked out the underground caves and seen how badly the place is flooded. He's looking for you, lass, and you'd best let him find you before that she-witch does or there's no telling what might happen.*

She whirled around, but she was alone in the storm. What good could a ghost do against such fierce winds, anyway?

"Where is he?" She spoke the words out loud, but the wind screamed her into silence. It didn't matter. She was asking the ghosts, and they heard her without words.

Look in the garage, Da said. *Where else do you think a man would find himself?*

Katie plastered herself against the stone wall of the mansion as another evil gust came up, threatening to knock her off her feet. If the situation weren't quite so desperate she might have been able to laugh. Even enchanted, ghost-ridden creatures tended to be ominously male when it came to cars and tools.

She'd grown so used to the constant shrieking of

the wind that the sudden, comparative quiet of the garage once she slammed the door was unnerving. It was very dark in there, but she saw him almost immediately, leaning over the engine of the Range Rover.

For a moment she froze. After all that had happened in the past hour, she was suddenly, curiously loath to face him. The last time she'd looked in his eyes he'd been buried deep inside her body, making love to her.

And then he'd abandoned her.

She didn't think he knew she was standing there, and she was in no particular mood to alert him, when he spoke without looking up. "Someone left the key turned on," he said in a cool, emotionless voice. "The battery was run way down, but I should be able to get it working. I'm going to have Willie drive you into town."

"You can't."

He raised his head to look at her then. The same, exquisitely beautiful face, the same haunted eyes. She didn't know how to reach him, and she was beyond trying.

"You have to leave, Katie," he said, his voice tight and controlled. "I can't give you anything you need, surely you can see that? The sooner you get out of here, the better. Willie's a decent driver— he'll get you into town..."

"Willie's dead."

He just stared at her. "He can't be," he said flatly.

"Oh, he is, all right." Katie's voice was high-pitched, bordering on hysteria, but there was nothing she could do about it. "He was dragging me upstairs, telling me all about the horrible things he was going to do to me, how he was going to kill me, when your parents terrified him into falling down the flight of stairs. He smashed his skull in, among other things. He's very dead."

"My parents," he echoed, staring at her.

"Mrs. Marvel is looking for us. She's going to kill both of us if she can."

"Unless my parents conveniently decide to stop her, as well?" O'Neal murmured in a dry, disbelieving voice. "Don't do this, Katie. I don't know whether what you're saying are lies or pathetic fantasies, I only know that Mrs. Marvel wouldn't hurt a living soul, and there are no such things as ghosts."

"No such things as creatures who change from man to beast at will, either?" she asked him.

He didn't even blink. "I'll drive you to town myself," he said. "You need to get away from this place, and then you'll realize how ridiculous all of this is."

"She's not going anywhere."

Mrs. Marvel's down-East voice was as warm and cozy as ever. She was standing at the far end of the garage, her tightly bound gray hair mussed from the incessant wind, her flowered rayon housedress soaked with rain. And blood.

She held a gun in her hand, a large, nasty one. And she looked very dangerous indeed.

O'Neal straightened slowly, staring at her through the murky light, staring at the gun. "Mrs. Marvel..." he said.

"Willie's dead, you know," Mrs. Marvel said. "That bitch probably told you already, but you probably didn't believe a word she said. You don't have much sense when it comes to the real world, O'Neal. You don't seem to realize how it operates. Money rules."

"Money?"

"That's why I'm here. That's why my boy and I have always been here. You bring in treasures and we remove the best of them. But you're not going to be bringing up more jewels from the sea, are you? And my boy's dead. She killed him."

"It was the ghosts..."

"Shut your face!" Mrs. Marvel hissed. "Don't you be giving me none of your lies. I've lived with that idiot boy of mine, telling me his stupid tales of sea creatures and such. I'm not going to start hearing about ghosts, as well."

"I didn't kill Willie, Mrs. Marvel," Katie said urgently, knowing that gun was pointed directly at her now. "I'm so sorry..."

"I'm not. He's been a trial to me for the last twelve years, more trouble than he was worth. But you've taken care of that, haven't you? I don't have to worry about anyone anymore.'' She chuckled, so softly the sound barely carried over the screaming wind.

"What are you going to do with us?'' O'Neal hadn't moved from behind the car, and he seemed almost unnaturally calm in the face of murder.

"Kill you, of course. You're going to take a nice walk to the cliffs and jump over, the pair of you. At least you'll get to die in each other's arms, like Romeo and Juliet. Until the sea tears you away from each other.'' She laughed again. "I'll have to do something about dragging Willie's body down there, as well, but I'll wait till this storm passes. He always was a big boy, and I don't fancy trudging out in the rain.''

"But the storm will wash any traces of blood away,'' O'Neal pointed out helpfully.

"True enough. But no one's going to be coming out here checking on things. You've made it clear that no one's welcome. I'll go into town next week for supplies, same as usual, and tell them everything's just fine. And then I'll take my own sweet time, packing up whatever's handy, before I leave this place for the good life.''

"Which you so richly deserve,'' O'Neal murmured.

"I could shoot you now,'' Mrs. Marvel snarled.

"Then you'd have to drag me to the cliffs.''

"I could leave you here to rot. As a matter of fact, I don't see why I don't do it…"

"If we drown there won't be evidence of foul play, and they'll be less likely to come after you," O'Neal said casually. "If the authorities find bullet-riddled corpses they're going to start wondering what happened to you, and they're going to be making a real effort to find you."

"Ah, you're a clever man, O'Neal," Mrs. Marvel murmured. "I hope you don't think you have a chance in hell of surviving out there. It's a full-blown hurricane. You'll drown, and your girlfriend with you, and chances are they'll never find what's left of your bodies."

"But if they do, wouldn't it be better if we didn't have any bullet holes in us?" he persisted.

"Much better." She gestured with the gun. "Come along, then. It's been a busy morning, and I haven't had my second cup of coffee. Let's finish this so I can relax."

Katie stared at her with horrified fascination. "What about Willie?"

Mrs. Marvel smiled at her. "He won't be needing any coffee, dearie."

Katie stood frozen, unable to move, when O'Neal came up beside her and took her hand in his. His skin was cold, as well, but the strength of his grip took her out of her sickened torpor to look up at him.

"It'll be all right," he said gently.

Mrs. Marvel's coarse laugh echoed through the garage. "That it will, dearie. You'll be in a better place than this vale of tears. Come along with you." And she gestured ahead of her with the gun.

Katie walked with O'Neal, taking odd comfort in the tight grip of his hand, and she didn't flinch when he pushed open the door. The wind caught it and flung it back against the building, filling the stall with the hurricane's fury.

"There's a banshee out there, Mrs. Marvel," he said, raising his voice above the noise of the storm.

"What's that?"

"A creature of the dead. She comes to collect lost souls, and she wails outside the windows where death comes calling."

"Then she's come to the right place," Mrs. Marvel replied tartly. "She'll have her hands full with Willie and the two of you. I don't imagine she'll want to waste her time with a sweet, harmless old woman like me. Keep moving."

They could barely stand beneath the force of the wind. O'Neal put his arm around her, pulling her tight against his body, and headed out into the storm, and Katie had no choice but to stay with him. Within the shelter of his body she couldn't see Mrs. Marvel, she could only hope the fierce wind would grab her squat, evil body and toss her into the ocean, but she doubted providence would be that kind. Mrs. Marvel was firmly of this earth, and it would take more than a hurricane to blow her vicious presence away.

She could feel the beat of his heart next to her face, rapid but steady. Beneath the cold and wet she could feel the warmth of him, the strength of him, and it brought her an irrational sense of peace. She wanted to call out to the ghosts, but she didn't say a word. What could they do? Mrs. Marvel wouldn't be frightened into falling as her son had. Mrs. Marvel wouldn't even see them.

Katie tripped, almost sprawling in the mud, but O'Neal caught her, pulling her up again, his hands strong and gentle. She couldn't even see his face through the blinding sheets of rain, she could only duck her head and cling to him as they made their endless trek to the sea.

Suddenly he stopped, gripping her tightly, and she felt his hand on her hair, pushing it away from her rain-soaked face.

She had the momentary hope that Mrs. Marvel had lost her way, had tripped and fallen beneath the force of the wind. And then she heard the roar.

The sea was like an angry beast, hungry for human sacrifice. The noise of it was deafening, terrifying, and she looked up at him in despair, knowing his face was the last thing she would see.

He cupped her face with his hands and put his mouth against hers. "I love you," he said. "Trust me."

She couldn't hear those words beneath the howl

of the storm, but she heard them in her heart, and she nodded blindly.

Mrs. Marvel was screaming at them, the words swallowed by the wind, and there was the crack of a gun being fired. O'Neal wrapped his arms around Katie, wrapped his body tightly against hers.

And together they went over the cliff, down, down, into the mouth of the hungry sea.

SHE COULDN'T BREATHE, but it didn't matter. Water surrounded her: icy, icy water, slapping at her, dragging at her, and she was alone. The cruel storm had ripped O'Neal away from her clinging arms, and she was alone in the ocean, and she was going to die.

It was so cold. So very cold and black, and she knew she should simply swallow that water and give in. Fighting would only prolong it. What had Fiona told her—drowning was a peaceful way to go? This didn't seem the slightest bit peaceful, it was cold and terrifying and she didn't want to die.

Something brushed past her, and she hit at it in terror. It knocked against her again, thrown against her by the force of the storm, and she struggled.

Don't fight it. Fiona's voice, in her head. *Put your arms around him.*

Around whom? She couldn't even see in the blackness of the sea, but this time when the large object knocked against her she didn't fight back, she reached out.

It was the seal, sleek and strongly muscled. And she wrapped her arms around his neck, barely realizing what she was doing. A moment later they had reached the surface, and she took in deep, painful gulps of air, choking as the waves sent more water down her throat.

He was a strong swimmer, her seal, but the force of the hurricane was powerful, too, and she wondered whether they would die together. She tried to see how far from shore they were, whether there was any chance they could make it back to safety, but through the sheets of rain things looked strange, ravaged, and she had no sense of where they were.

Hold tight to him, Fiona said. And Katie held on. Tightly. Trusting. Knowing who it was.

The noise around her was deafening. The scream of the wind tore at her, and she wanted to close her eyes and scream, as well, when a new noise, deep and thunderous, rose above the wail of the storm.

She looked up, just in time to see the sharp jut of land collapse into the sea with a roar so powerful that the very ocean shook with it, taking the house and everything with it. The wave of water caught them and hurtled them beneath the surface again, rolling over and over, and all she could do was cling to her seal, bury her face against his wet, sleek hide and hold on.

Time disappeared. The icy water had taken her beyond pain, beyond numbness, into a strange shadow world of fog and ice. Her mind barely functioned, and she was grateful. She knew his body was strong and powerful, and she knew that she had to keep her arms locked around his neck, no matter what. If she did nothing else, she had to somehow keep her grip, even when she could no longer feel her hands, her arms, feel any part of her body but the warm animal hide of the seal beneath her.

He would take care of her, and she would let him. This time she couldn't save herself, she had to let go and allow someone else to take the burden. She had to give herself to him, more deeply than she had last night. Last night she had given him her body. Today, in the cold dark death of the storm-chased ocean, she gave him her soul.

She dreamed. She thought she must have died. All around her the sea grew more peaceful, and roses seemed to float beside her. It was darker than ever, and while the waves still slapped at her, her head was now sheltered from the incessant rain. She could hear it in the distance, but she was protected now, and she sighed, ready to release her death grip, ready to sink beneath the icy waves and dream forever.

His nose was cold, wet and whiskery as it jabbed into her back, and she opened her eyes in shock as she started to slip beneath the surface. They were in some sort of cave, and the seal was nudging her, no, shoving her, toward a shallow ledge just above the rising water.

She used the last of her energy to swim to the

rim, clinging to it with numb hands. But there was no way she would be able to pull herself up onto it.

Her frozen hands slipped, and she went under the water, coming back up sputtering. "I can't," she said.

The seal was barely a foot away from her, floating in the icy water with effortless grace, watching her. There was no censure in his eyes, just patience.

She tried again, scraping her hands along the sharp rock as she slid back down. She wanted to cry, but she was past that, and she didn't want to die sniveling like a baby, like a weak, helpless ninny.

She turned and looked at the seal. She could drown, and he would drown with her. She knew he would. It was almost impossible for a seal to drown—they could stay underwater for ages—but this one would manage it. If she didn't do something to get herself out of the death-grip of the icy sea.

She looked into his feral eyes. "Help me, Jamie," she said, her voice hoarse from the salt water. "Get me out of here."

A moment later he disappeared beneath the dark, churning water, smooth and graceful. And gone.

He erupted beneath her, and her body exploded from the water as the seal's bunched muscles propelled her. She landed on the stone ledge, hard, banging her hip and knee, smashing her elbow, and she didn't care. She was free from the sucking stranglehold of the carnivorous ocean, and all she could do was cling to the solid rock and weep.

Chapter Sixteen

It was a long time before she realized he was there, sitting at the far end of the narrow ledge. A pile of wet clothes lay on the ledge beside him, but he was naked, his head buried in his arms.

She barely had enough strength to pull herself upright, and she was afraid he would ignore her. The water was lapping close to the edge of the stone shelf, and it narrowed and led off deeper into the cave, into water and darkness, with no visible escape. As far as Katie could see, they hadn't cheated death. They'd only postponed it.

It was quiet in the cave, hushed and still. O'Neal lifted his head to look at her, and even in the darkness she could see the wariness in his eyes.

She wanted to touch him, to cross the few feet that separated them, but there was an invisible shield around him, keeping her away. So she had to make do with words.

"How?" she asked, trying to keep her voice

from shaking with the cold. "How could it be possible?"

He didn't pretend to misunderstand her. He simply shook his head. "I don't know. No one knows. It doesn't happen very often. Every fourth or fifth generation one of us is born, and there's no warning, no reason. Just the curse of the sea, visited on the dark O'Neals."

"Curse?" she echoed, shivering. "I'd think of it more as a gift."

She might as well have told him she was the Virgin Mary. He stared at her in astonishment. "Gift?" he echoed in disbelief.

"Of course," she said. "We'd both be dead right now if it weren't for your gift and the fact that Mrs. Marvel is too unimaginative to believe in such things."

"It didn't do my family any good."

"Oh, Jamie," she cried. "It did. It kept you alive, to love and remember them. To go on with your own life. You couldn't save them, but you saved me. Twice. I don't imagine they'd think it a fair trade..."

He lifted his head to look at her through the dim light, and he smiled faintly. "And what does my ghostly family have to tell you about that?"

Fiona's voice danced in her head. *This is the way it's supposed to be, Katie. Whether we like it or not, this is what's right. You're the one he'll spend his life with, grow old with, have babies with. We're long dead, and it's past time he let us go.*

She was shaking from the cold so hard she thought her bones would rattle through her skin. "They say it's all right," she said. Except that the words came out shattered with her uncontrollable shivering.

He crossed the narrow ledge to her. "I know," he said. "Deep in my heart, I know."

"Are we going to die?"

"No." His voice was firm.

"People die from hypothermia, you know," she said between her chattering teeth.

"You won't. I'll warm you." He began unfastening the buttons on her sodden shirt, and she stared at him in disbelief as he slowly, methodically stripped the clothes away from her. His hands were warm against her icy skin.

"You think this will help?" she gasped, as the cold air hit her wet skin.

His smile was slow and utterly mesmerizing. "I can think of only one way to warm you. I'll simply have to make the ultimate sacrifice and make love to you."

"No," she said, panicked, as he reached for the fastening of her jeans.

He paused, looking up at her. "No?"

"I can't do it," she said in her shivery, miserable voice. "I can't have sex with you again. I can't make love with a man who doesn't love me, even to save my life.''

His smile was slow and sultry, and immediately the heat began to build. "Then we don't have a problem," he said, and pulled her cold, half-naked body into his arms.

He was warm. For the first time he was the bringer of heat and fire, warming her, bringing life back to her chilled skin, melting the ice that seemed to encase her. He kissed her, and his mouth was cold and wet, like the sea, and she wanted more. Everywhere he touched her, heat followed, and she wanted to be naked with him, entwined with him, hot with him, burning up.

The rock ledge was hard beneath them, but she hardly noticed. His skin was wet and salty, and she pressed her mouth against his chest. His hands touched her everywhere, warming her, setting her on fire. She reached for him, her hands clumsy and desperate in her need, and he covered her, like a blanket of fire.

She was shaking, shivering, hot and cold at the same time, and he was life, burning. She wanted to crawl inside him, to lose herself in his heat. He caught her hand in his, lowering it to his body, and the smooth, silken strength of him was something she needed. She arched up to meet him, closing her eyes, hearing the distant storm roaring in her ears, the water lapping around them, and she was floating in a warm, glorious sea of delight.

His first thrust joined them completely, and she wanted to cry out, but there were no words. She could only lie beneath him, taking him, giving to him, shaking with a storm of emotion more powerful than the hurricane that battered them.

She clung to him, tightly, her face buried against his shoulder, breathing in the scent of him, the feel of him. And the first wave that hit her body was sharp and fierce, a convulsion of fire, endless, eternal.

And he joined her, filling her with life, filling her with the sea, filling her emptiness; and her hot tears warmed them both.

His body was wrapped tightly around hers, and he stroked her damp skin with infinite tenderness, kissing her mouth, when suddenly he stilled. "You don't suppose they're watching us, do you?" he asked.

The thought had already occurred to Katie. "I don't think so."

"Because I'd hate to think my family had turned into voyeurs as well as ghosts," he murmured, kissing the side of her neck. "You taste like the ocean."

"So do you." She wanted to taste more of him. She wanted to push him onto his back and taste him everywhere, but the rock was too hard and the water was rising higher. She touched his face. "Are we going to die together?" she asked softly.

"Yes," he said with calm assurance. "But not

for another fifty or sixty years at the very least. We have to get out of here before the water gets any higher.''

"How?"

He shook his head. "I don't know. I've never explored this particular cave and I have no idea how secure it is. We have to be somewhere under the main section of land—it looked to me as if the entire outcropping of land went into the sea along with the house. Maybe we're somewhere near the guest house.'' He was pulling on his wet clothes with a complete disregard for their cold, wet condition, and Katie reluctantly followed suit. Either way she was freezing to death, and the wet clothes offered her some protection from the wind.

O'Neal rose, moving deeper into the cave, and Katie scrambled to feet, peering into the darkness. "Do you suppose Mrs. Marvel could have survived?"

O'Neal looked back her. "No," he said. "I saw her body.''

Katie thought about it, trying to summon up sorrow. She failed utterly. "Good," she said finally. "I hope the fishes eat her.''

"They'd probably get sick," O'Neal said lightly. "We have a choice, Katie love. We either try to get out this way, or we go back into the sea.''

Katie shivered. "I vote for staying dry."

"We could be trapped. These caves might collapse, as well. If we swim for it I could keep you safe. At least for a while.''

She wasn't sure if she liked that ''at least for a while'' bit, but she decided not to mention that. ''I trust you, O'Neal,'' she said. ''I'll go where you want me to go.''

His smile was crooked. ''You'll follow me to the ends of the earth, will you?'' The water was up over the ledge now, and he looked back into the darkness of the cave. She moved behind him, putting her arms around his waist, resting her head against his wet shirt, listening to the solid feel of his heartbeat.

She felt the sudden rigidity of his body before she saw the light. She backed away, just enough to see Fiona, floating in the distance, holding her small, pale hand out to her brother.

''This way, Jamie,'' Fiona said.

And O'Neal, who'd never seen or heard the ghosts, reached out with his hand to touch her.

IN THE END he thought he'd imagined her. The pale, sweet face of his sister, the hand held out to him. He'd touched her, another dream, and known that everything was going to be all right.

And then Fiona was gone forever, and there was Katie, who had somehow become dearer to him than all the world, holding his hand and trusting him as he led her out of the caves that honeycombed the cliffs, led her to the shelter of the old guest house.

It was easy enough to break through the boarded-up front door, and the house was safe and dry inside. He pulled the holland covers off the furniture and carried Katie up to one of the bedrooms, stripping off their clothes and wrapping them up in the dusty linen covers, just holding her tightly in his arms until they slept.

In his dreams he heard them. His mother's voice, warm, tender, lilting. *They'll make lovely babies, Seamus.*

And his father, bawdy and charming as ever, his voice thick with Ireland. *And not a flipper among them, I'll wager. I wonder if our Katie knows that.*

She knows, Seamus. She knows.

And then there was silence. No more voices. No more wind. No thunderous rain beating against the old wooden house. He opened his eyes and saw weak sunlight through the boarded-up windows, and he loved Katie into wakefulness, then dozy desire, and then shattering pleasure.

They stepped out into the fitful light of early dawn. The storm that had plagued them had been swept out to sea. So had the huge stone house and the outcropping of land it had sat on. It was warm, an Indian summer day, and Katie Flynn leaned back in his arms with an accepting sigh.

He thought of all the things he should ask her. All the things he should tell her. Plans for the future, how they'd survive, what he'd seen and heard.

But he said nothing. There would be time for

that. Days and weeks and years, stretching out ahead of them. He'd have time enough to tell her everything.

Time enough to love.

Epilogue

Ten years later, the guest house

Katie was perched precariously on a ladder, paint-brush in hand, when O'Neal came charging through the door. "What the hell are you doing up there in your condition?" he thundered.

She loved it when he yelled. O'Neal was a man of grand passion, and he had a habit of yelling when he was most strongly moved.

"The platform's secure," she said calmly. "I want to finish this mural before the baby comes."

"Why can't you paint on canvas like a sensible woman?" he demanded, coming to the bottom of the ladder and glowering up at her.

"I could. Once I finish with the house. But they'll need to be very large canvasses. I like to work on a grand scale." She smiled down at him.

"You have green paint on your nose," he said gruffly.

Without hesitation she leaned over and swiped a

line of green paint along his cheekbone. "Now we match."

"The girls will be home soon," he said with a meaningful gleam in his beautiful eyes. "So you know you're safe for the time being."

"But they'll go to bed sooner or later."

"Fiona wants to have a friend over for the night."

Katie sighed. "Maeve is such a pain in the butt when Fiona has friends."

"So why are we having another one? Aren't two girls enough?" he demanded, knowing the answer full well. He reached out and touched her round belly, and the baby kicked at his hand.

"More than enough," Katie agreed, "but Seamus here has other ideas."

"It'll be another girl," O'Neal warned her.

"So you always say. And I'm telling you it's a boy. I know he's male. I've had the worst morning sickness I've ever had. He's already oppressing me, like the rest of your gender."

O'Neal leaned up and kissed her, a brief, deep kiss on the mouth. "Poor, abused creature," he murmured against her mouth. "You'll have to teach me the error of my ways."

Her eyes were alight with happiness. "I'll do that, O'Neal."

She climbed down the ladder, O'Neal hovering behind her, and she admired the painting with a critical eye. It was an underwater scene, full of fanciful fishes and dazzling mermaids with her daughters' faces. In the shadowy reaches lurked a seal, watching over them all. "I think this one is my masterpiece," she said.

"And I think you're mad," he said. "To live out here alone with me and spend your life painting."

"And raising babies. And fixing up this old house. And simply living life. Mad, indeed, Jamie," she said cheerfully. She put her arms around his neck, resting against him peacefully. "What about you, my love? Why are you still here?"

He smiled down at her. "This is where I belong. I can't think of a better place to be."

"Lucky for you," she murmured. "I have your family on my side. You misbehave and I'll sic the ghosts on you."

"They're gone," he said, kissing her eyelids with erotic tenderness. "You know as well as I do that they've been gone for ten years."

Katie didn't bother to correct him. He wasn't the one who'd watched her children have long, cheerful conversations with their grandpa and their aunt Fiona, he wasn't the one who'd seen an invisible, soothing, grandmotherly hand brush Maeve's soft red hair.

"Of course they are, love," she said cheerfully.

And somewhere in the distance she heard a faint, ghostly laugh.

HARLEQUIN®

AMERICAN ◆ ROMANCE®

COMING NEXT MONTH

**Next month, celebrate Christmas with American Romance
as we take you
HOME FOR THE HOLIDAYS**

#705 CHRISTMAS IN THE COUNTRY by Muriel Jensen
Now that he was free, ex-hostage Jeff James wanted nothing more than
to eat Liza deLane's glazed ham for Christmas. But for the woman
touted as the "new Martha Stewart," the *timing* couldn't be worse. She
had a borrowed husband, rented kids...and a very big problem!

#706 MARLEY AND HER SCROOGE by Emily Dalton
When Carl Merrick fell asleep at his desk on Christmas Eve, his business
partner Marley Jacobs made an unexpected appearance in his dreams.
Dressed in a baby-doll nightie, she warned him to change his Scroogelike
ways by the stroke of midnight or someone else would be sharing her
Christmas future.

#707 BELLS, RINGS & ANGELS' WINGS by Linda Randall Wisdom
One minute Libby Barnes idly wished she didn't have to spend Christmas
with her family; the next she wished she'd kept her mouth shut. Because
there was her house, there were her parents, there was her husband Ty—
but nobody knew who *she* was....

#708 THE SANTA SUIT by Karen Toller Whittenburg
Single mom Kate Harmon had always told her twins the truth—
Santa Claus didn't exist. So why had they hired detective Gabe Housley
to find him? And why was Kate hoping that Gabe was Santa's answer to
the twins' request for a daddy?

AVAILABLE THIS MONTH:

#701 IN PAPA BEAR'S BED
Judy Christenberry

#703 OVERNIGHT WIFE
Mollie Molay

#702 A DARK & STORMY NIGHT
Anne Stuart

#704 MISTER CHRISTMAS
Linda Cajio

Look us up on-line at: http://www.romance.net

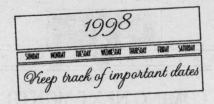

1998

SUNDAY   MONDAY   TUESDAY   WEDNESDAY   THURSDAY   FRIDAY   SATURDAY

Keep track of important dates

Three beautiful and colorful calendars that celebrate some of the most popular trends in America today.

Look for:

Just Babies—a 16 month calendar that features a full year of absolutely adorable babies!

Hometown Quilts—a 16 month calendar featuring quilted art squares, plus a short history on twelve different quilt patterns.

Inspirations—a 16 month calendar with inspiring pictures and quotations.

Steeple Hill™

 HARLEQUIN®

Value priced at $9.99 U.S./$11.99 CAN., these calendars make a perfect gift!

Available in retail outlets in August 1997.

CAL98

DEBBIE MACOMBER

invites you to the

HEART OF TEXAS

Join Debbie Macomber as she brings you the lives
and loves of the folks in the ranching community
of Promise, Texas.

If you loved Midnight Sons—don't miss
Heart of Texas! A brand-new six-book series
from Debbie Macomber.

Available in February 1998
at your favorite retail store.

Heart of Texas by Debbie Macomber

Lonesome Cowboy	February '98
Texas Two-Step	March '98
Caroline's Child	April '98
Dr. Texas	May '98
Nell's Cowboy	June '98
Lone Star Baby	July '98

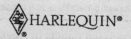

HARLEQUIN®

HPHRT1

Free Gift Offer

With a Free Gift proof-of-purchase
from any Harlequin® book, you can receive
a beautiful cubic zirconia pendant.

This stunning marquise-shaped stone is a genuine cubic
zirconia—accented by an 18" gold tone necklace.
(Approximate retail value $19.95)

Send for yours today...
compliments of HARLEQUIN®

To receive your free gift, a cubic zirconia pendant, send us one original proof-of-purchase, photocopies not accepted, from the back of any Harlequin Romance®, Harlequin Presents®, Harlequin Temptation®, Harlequin Superromance®, Harlequin Intrigue®, Harlequin American Romance®, or Harlequin Historicals® title available at your favorite retail outlet, together with the Free Gift Certificate, plus a check or money order for $1.65 U.S./$2.15 CAN. (do not send cash) to cover postage and handling, payable to Harlequin Free Gift Offer. We will send you the specified gift. Allow 6 to 8 weeks for delivery. Offer good until December 31, 1997, or while quantities last. Offer valid in the U.S. and Canada only.

Free Gift Certificate

Name: _____

Address: _____

City: _____ State/Province: _____ Zip/Postal Code: _____

Mail this certificate, one proof-of-purchase and a check or money order for postage and handling to: HARLEQUIN FREE GIFT OFFER 1997. In the U.S.: 3010 Walden Avenue, P.O. Box 9071, Buffalo NY 14269-9057. In Canada: P.O. Box 604, Fort Erie, Ontario L2Z 5X3.

FREE GIFT OFFER   084-KEZ
ONE PROOF-OF-PURCHASE
To collect your fabulous FREE GIFT, a cubic zirconia pendant, you must include this
original proof-of-purchase for each gift with the properly completed Free Gift Certificate.

084-KEZR

HARLEQUIN WOMEN KNOW ROMANCE WHEN THEY SEE IT.

And they'll see it on **ROMANCE CLASSICS**, the new 24-hour TV channel devoted to romantic movies and original programs like the special **Romantically Speaking—Harlequin™ Goes Prime Time**.

Romantically Speaking—Harlequin™ Goes Prime Time introduces you to many of your favorite romance authors in a program developed exclusively for Harlequin® readers.

Watch for **Romantically Speaking—Harlequin™ Goes Prime Time** beginning in the summer of 1997.

If you're not receiving **ROMANCE CLASSICS**, call your local cable operator or satellite provider and ask for it today!

Escape to the network of your dreams.

See Ingrid Bergman and Gregory Peck in *Spellbound* on Romance Classics.

FREE BOOK OFFER!

**With every Harlequin Ultimate Guides™ order,
receive a FREE bonus book!**

#80507	HOW TO TALK TO A NAKED MAN	$4.99 U.S. ☐	$5.50 CAN. ☐
#80508	I CAN FIX THAT	$5.99 U.S. ☐	$6.99 CAN. ☐
#80510	WHAT YOUR TRAVEL AGENT KNOWS THAT YOU DON'T	$5.99 U.S. ☐	$6.99 CAN. ☐
#80511	RISING TO THE OCCASION More Than Manners: Real Life Etiquette for Today's Woman	$5.99 U.S. ☐	$6.99 CAN. ☐
#80513	WHAT GREAT CHEFS KNOW THAT YOU DON'T	$5.99 U.S. ☐	$6.99 CAN. ☐
#80514	WHAT SAVVY INVESTORS KNOW THAT YOU DON'T	$5.99 U.S. ☐	$6.99 CAN. ☐

(quantities may be limited on some titles)

TOTAL AMOUNT	$
POSTAGE & HANDLING	$
($1.00 for one book, 50¢ for each additional)	
APPLICABLE TAXES*	$ _____
TOTAL PAYABLE	$ _____

(check or money order—please do not send cash)

*New York residents remit applicable sales taxes.
Canadian residents remit applicable GST and provincial taxes.

To order, complete this form and send it, along with a check or money order for the total above, payable to Harlequin Ultimate Guides, to: **In the U.S.:** 3010 Walden Avenue, P.O. Box 9047, Buffalo, NY 14269-9047; **In Canada:** P.O. Box 613, Fort Erie, Ontario, L2A 5X3.

HARLEQUIN ULTIMATE GUIDES™
What women really want to know!

Official Proof of Purchase

Please send me my FREE bonus book with this order.

Name: _____

Address: _____

City: _____

State/Prov:. _____ Zip/Postal Code: _____

Reader Service Acct.#: _____ **KFZ**

Look us up on-line at: http://www.romance.net

NFPOP